THE MONKEY THIEF

The MONKEY THIEF

Aileen Kilgore Henderson

Paul Mirocha
ILLUSTRATOR

SCHOLASTIC INC.

New York   Toronto   London   Auckland   Sydney
Mexico City   New Delhi   Hong Kong   Buenos Aires

Cover design by Gail Wallinga.
Interior design by Will Powers.
The text of this book is set in Stone Serif.

Text copyright © 1996 by Aileen Kilgore Henderson.
Illustrations copyright © 1996 by Paul Mirocha.
All rights reserved. Published by Scholastic Inc., 557 Broadway, New York, NY 10012, by arrangement with Milkweed Editions.
Printed in the U.S.A.

ISBN 0-439-57685-7

9 10   40   12 11

To Anne and Patrick

I could not have written this book without the help of my daughter, Anne Henderson Weston, who lives with her husband, Patrick, in the Costa Rican rain forest. Many of the things that happen to Steve in *The Monkey Thief* first happened to Anne and Patrick.

Thanks also to J. Selwyn Hollingsworth, Ph.D., Department of Anthropology, University of Alabama, Tuscaloosa, who has lived and traveled in Costa Rica, and who read my manuscript and offered suggestions.

THE MONKEY THIEF

CHAPTER ONE

THE BIG PLANE touched down on the
runway of the San José airport,
gradually braking its speed as it bumped along toward the terminal. Steve Hanson pressed his face
against the window for his first look at Costa Rica.
Only hours ago he had left Minnesota in the snow
and ice of January. Now from the window he could
see the sunshine and blossoms of a different world.
How he came to be here, ready to deplane to meet
his uncle Matt, was beyond understanding. One day
he was comfortably established in his do-nothing
lifestyle. The next day, it seemed, he was winging
his way south to visit his uncle who was setting up
a nature preserve in the rain forest with some Costa
Rican friends.

"We plan to have students come here to study,"
Uncle Matt wrote Mom and Dad right after
Christmas. "My partners travel and raise money
for our project while I live in the forest and take care
of it. I have to build a house while we're having the
dry season. That doesn't give me much time. Will
Steve come help? Of course, I'd like to have Jennifer

too, but I thought she'd rather come after the students arrive. Besides, she's so busy showing that champion horse and winning all those ribbons! Congratulations, Jennie! Hoping the answer is 'yes' from all of you, I'm enclosing Steve's ticket."

"He's just a couch potato," Steve's older sister said when she heard the letter. "He can't build anything."

"Now, now, Jennifer," Grandma reproved her. "Steve could do a lot of things."

In the pause that followed, Steve knew that everyone was silently adding, *"If* he only would!"

"It's a great opportunity," Dad beamed.

"We'll talk to your teacher," Mom added, her eyes shining. "Sometimes the school approves of leave for foreign travel."

"Why me?" Steve had asked, reluctant. In all of his twelve years, he had never left his home state of Minnesota.

"You're his namesake," Dad said. "Stephen Matthew. That makes you special to Matt."

That surprised Steve. Nobody else seemed to think him special. In fact, everyone acted disappointed in him. At family get-togethers, his great-aunts and great-uncles looked over their spectacles at him where he sat, minding his own business, and demanded, "Cat got your tongue, Steve? Say something!" His cousins tried to get him to play ball, but the sun was too hot and the ants bit him, and he didn't see any sense to their quarreling and name-calling.

No matter how hard he tried, Steve could never measure up to what others expected. He finally gave up trying. He stayed in his room out of everybody's way as much as he could, watching television and munching on snacks.

But that worried Grandpa. "He doesn't do anything. He doesn't say anything. Is he sick?"

"He's okay," Grandma said, putting her arm around Steve, who just stood there. "One of these days he'll catch fire for something. Then watch out!" She rolled her eyes and made a sound like a siren.

Steve didn't know what Grandma meant when she said he'd catch fire someday, but he didn't think much about it. Maybe it had something to do with "communicating." That was a word he heard too often. His report card usually had some note on it about communicating—"Steve needs to learn to communicate," or "Steve lacks communication skills." Even when his parents came to school to confer about his trip, he overheard his teacher say, "In a strange country, Steve will be forced to communicate."

He sighed now, remembering. Why was communicating such a big deal? And did his uncle truly think he was special? Sometimes he suspected that his family and the school and Uncle Matt had ganged up on him, shipping him off to this place he never wanted to be. But, as always before, he found it easier to go along with their plans than to resist. He hoped he'd recognize this uncle who supposedly thought he was "special." Would Uncle Matt, like the others, end up being disappointed with him?

When the seat belt light blinked off and the plane door scraped open, the passengers leaped up as one unit and crowded into the aisle, struggling with their bags and boxes. Steve stayed in place, lost in a confusion of thoughts and in no hurry to face Uncle Matt. At last the narrow aisle cleared. Dragging his flight bag from under the seat, he trudged toward the door. He had in hand the special documents allowing him to stay in the country for eight months, and after claiming his baggage, he cleared customs without any delay.

Uncle Matt was waiting, beaming just like Dad. Steve hesitated, wondering if he should offer to shake hands. Before he could make up his mind, his uncle folded him in a great bear hug, saying, "Welcome to Costa Rica! How you've grown! No more little Stevie—you're big Steve now!"

Uncle Matt led him to the parking lot where he singled out an old red truck loaded to the brim. "Building supplies for the house," he explained, shoving around boxes and boards to make room for Steve's baggage. "We'll be living in a tent until the house is finished."

"Okay," Steve agreed, squeezing into the passenger side among boxes of groceries.

They headed south on what turned out to be a long day's trip to the Pacific side of Costa Rica. On the way Steve glimpsed a country of smiling people who talked in musical Spanish; of decorated ox carts with wooden wheels that sang as they turned; of wide rivers that had to be crossed on ferries; and, toward the end of the trip, Steve saw the rain forest, dark with foliage and loud with many kinds of cries and calls.

Once Uncle Matt gestured toward the horizon. "See that? Slash and burn!"

In all directions the land looked like war zones Steve had seen on television—every growing thing destroyed and blackened.

"This is where the trees were cut and burned. Nothing was left to keep the topsoil from washing away when the heavy rains came. The streams filled with mud and gradually dried up, killing the fish. Other animals and birds couldn't find food or shelter, so they either died or went away. We don't want that to happen to our forest."

Steve looked but could think of nothing to say. The heavily loaded truck chugged up the hills at a walking pace and rolled only a smidgen faster down the hills. When they finally arrived as the sun was setting, Steve saw the tent first thing. It stood, small and slightly crooked, under the huge trees dangling with vines.

"Well, what do you think?" Uncle Matt asked expectantly, handing Steve a bag of groceries.

Steve shrugged. "It's all right."

Inside the tent was a jumble of all sorts of stuff— a table, a bench, a gas stove, a lantern, which Uncle Matt lighted—but nowhere did he see a bed of any kind. He was tired enough to flop down on one right now. He set the bag on the table and stood there.

"Where's my helper?" Uncle Matt called. Slowly Steve went out to finish unloading.

Later, they ate a supper of rough white cheese with cornmeal tortillas, and mangoes so ripe the juice dripped off Steve's elbows as he ate them.

It was then that Uncle Matt explained about the beds. There weren't any. Close to the tent, strung between trees, were two twine hammocks, looking like collapsed tennis nets.

"You'll soon adjust to sleeping this way," Uncle Matt said. "A hammock's better than a bed. It's cooler."

As they cleared the food from the table, he said, "We have to bring our water from the spring. Will you make sure we always have water for drinking and dish washing?"

"All right."

"In fact, you may want to take charge of the tent. My crew and I want to finish the roof and the outside of the house before the heavy rains begin, so I won't have much time for chores. Are you willing to be chief-cook-and-bottle-washer?"

Steve agreed—that was the easiest thing to do—though he had no inkling what Uncle Matt meant.

He soon learned. Each morning Uncle Matt got him up at dawn to help with breakfast. Then he went off to work on the house near the ocean, leaving Steve with the tent to clean. At times, when his uncle came home at noon, he found Steve still struggling with chores and lunch not ready.

"I know it's all strange to you," Uncle Matt said, "but keep trying. You'll catch on." He sounded cheerful but looked a little strained as he pitched in to bring order out of the muddle Steve had made. "Putting things back on the shelf where you found them helps. Like the beans or the rice—they always stay here." He showed Steve. "Then you don't have to hunt around, and the work space stays clear."

Every day Steve had to take a pail and go along a path through the forest to a clearing where the spring flowed from under a fern-covered bank. If they used a lot of water in the tent, he had to go several times a day because the walk was too long and the water too heavy to bring more than one pail at a time.

"Not to worry," Uncle Matt laughed, playfully punching him in his bulging middle. "That flab will soon disappear."

Steve knew he was out of condition. Seeing the lean, muscular people here—not a couch potato among them—made him feel worse. But everything was so different, and the work seemed endless. Often he thought of quitting. What made him keep trying was Uncle Matt. He really wanted to please him.

Steve managed to eat beans and rice and use tortillas for bread every day, but sleeping in a hammock was impossible. It curved his body in a half-moon shape and swayed and rocked all night long. He felt seasick, lying awake for hours listening to the forest noises and Uncle Matt's deep breathing.

If he could just get used to the hammock and not tire out so quickly! The cooking part wasn't too hard, even though he still made mistakes—burned the beans or left the salt out of the rice. As the days passed, he realized that he could do only one thing right, yet there was a complication there, too.

CHAPTER TWO

THE ONE THING Steve did right was keeping the tent supplied with water for drinking, bathing, and cleaning the kitchen area. He had to make such frequent trips to the spring that his feet wore the path to dust. He was proud of the good job he did as water carrier, especially after he became a two-bucket carrier. The complication he had to cope with was don Luís, an elderly man who lived within sight of the spring. He always seemed to be watching for Steve to come along so he could talk.

"I use my English," don Luís said. "Pretty good English, yes?"

Steve shrugged, which was hard to do carrying a heavy bucket of water in each hand, and said, "It's all right."

Every day don Luís talked about different things, obviously trying to keep Steve with him. He invited Steve to his house to see his chickens, two only, he said, but very fine. He offered to take Steve to an *excelente* mango tree—"*muy delicioso,*" he assured him. Steve knew that the elderly man wanted him to talk back, but it was no use. Steve didn't have anything to say, and he had work waiting to be done back in the tent. He listened to don Luís, agreed with him when he had to, then hurried away.

The old man never gave up trying. One morning in great excitement he pointed up, up, to the high tree tops. Steve looked just to please him.

"Monkeys," don Luís said. *"Muy rapidos."*

They went so fast, they were cinnamon colored blurs among the branches. Steve kept looking, this time to please himself. Then he took the water to the tent.

When next he saw don Luís, he asked his first question since coming to Costa Rica.

"Those monkeys—what kind?"

"Squirrel monkeys." Don Luís's face shone with happiness. "You like them?"

"They're okay," Steve said.

Another day he asked don Luís, "Are there other monkeys besides squirrel?"

"Sí. In this forest also live the howlers—*muy grandes."* He used his hands to show they were large and then barked gruffly like a big dog with a bad cold. "Also the white-faced." He circled his face with the open palm of his hand and tousled his hair down over his eyes. "Also, when I was *un niño,* the spider monkeys lived here. Everyone wanted a spider monkey for the cooking pot." He smacked his wrinkled lips, adding, "Now they are gone."

Steve returned to the tent with his water pails. He began lunch preparation, following the instructions Uncle Matt jotted down each morning. He reheated red beans one of the carpenters had brought them, and rice, which today he mixed with slivers of fish left from last night. His uncle liked the rice to be colored yellow with *annatto,* a coloring from the seeds of a forest tree. Steve thought it looked pretty that way, but once he added too much of the margarine-like *annatto* and turned the rice red. That was embarrassing, but Uncle Matt joked about it, and Steve hadn't let it happen again.

Today, monkeys kept coming into his thoughts, especially what don Luís had said about the ones living in their forest. Until now the forest was nothing but a great mix of voices, day and night. Sometimes he felt deafened by the volume and intensity of the noise. He couldn't guess what made all that racket, but now he was determined to listen for the howlers that don Luís imitated.

Then the sounds began making sense. His ears quickly tuned in on the gruff barking of the big howlers. They awakened him at dawn with a clamor of coughing barks, and at day's end they set up such a roar nothing else could be heard. They sounded so close, he wanted to hike into the forest to find them.

"No, no," don Luís protested. "Big monkeys very loud, but very far."

"That howling's awful! What're they saying?"

"Many things. At sunrise they say *'buenos días'* to the world. At sunset they call the family together to go to their sleeping tree."

Steve paused and considered this. Thinking was something he'd been doing lately since he found out about monkeys.

He began speaking up and asking questions, too, because he realized that doing so was a way to find out some of the things he wanted to know. His words didn't always come out right, but don Luís was patient and waited until Steve could make his meaning clear. Steve tried to be as patient when don Luís couldn't express what he wanted to say in English.

He found that if he kept his mind on what he was doing, he could work faster. The quicker the tent chores got done, the sooner he could be outside where the monkeys were. Whenever he finished he grabbed a basket and rushed to meet don Luís at the spring. For the rest of the morning, they explored the forest and the clearings, picking fruit for lunch.

anona

carambola

caimitos

uvilla

Some were familiar to Steve—bananas, oranges, and lemons—but many of them he'd never heard of. His new friend had a name for all of them—*carambola,* which was shaped like a star when don Luís cut it cross-wise with his machete; *zapote, imbe, anona, uvilla*—Steve liked to say them over. They sampled each one that was ripe and filled the basket with those they liked. The *anona,* Steve's favorite, was the size of a cantaloupe, with yellow skin so wrinkled it resembled a relief map of Mars complete with canals. The custard inside tasted like lemon pie.

Don Luís's favorite came from the *carao* tree— brown pods filled with a goo that reminded Steve of used motor oil mixed with molasses. Often they came home sticky from head to toe, with Steve's basket overflowing. Don Luís stashed his harvest in a string bag that hung from his shoulder and stretched to fit however much he put into it. He told Steve that he wove it using a single-stick loom, and he promised to make such a bag for him. That way both of Steve's hands would be free for picking. What a lot more fun than going to the supermarket!

An odd and useful thing about don Luís was his machete. He never went anywhere without it swinging in a crude leather covering from a rope around his waist. What amazing things he could do with it! He could split open a coconut or probe for *yuca* roots, lop off the head of a fer-de-lance snake crossing the path. *"Muy peligroso,"* he said of the big brown snake. "Very dangerous."

Every so often, when they rested and talked on the hollow log in the shade of don Luís's yard, he took a small metal file he called a *lima* out of his pocket and sharpened the machete blade. It was a wicked looking thing, the size of the biggest knife in the kitchen back home, combined with the butcher's meat cleaver. When don Luís used the machete to chop a tree or cut brush, his movements were so smooth the machete was like a part of his arm.

On their journeys they sometimes heard monkeys chirruping, but the dense foliage hid them. Steve felt discouraged that he could never get a good look at a monkey. An idea was taking shape in his mind, a plan that he could not carry out unless he made friends with the monkeys.

One day he asked don Luís, "Won't the monkeys ever come out of the forest so I can see them?"

"*Sí.*" Don Luís's eyes twinkled. "You want a monkey of your own?"

Steve's jaw dropped. How did he guess? That was exactly his plan. A monkey would make the neatest pet ever. "But I can't decide which kind—that's why I need them to come out of the forest, so I can choose."

"I will tell you how," don Luís said. "Do many things outside. You will not see monkeys, but they will be watching. When you do something of interest to them, they will tell other monkeys, and all will come."

Steve thought over that advice. He started offering to do extra things for Uncle Matt—digging *yuca* roots from the garden, washing clothes in a tub at the spring, setting out young banana plants in the tent area. He made as much noise as he could while he worked—whistling, singing, banging—hoping to interest the monkeys and draw them out of the dense forest. At first, the loud sound of his voice startled him, and he felt silly, but then he remembered that the monkeys might be watching. Everything he did, he thought of the monkeys as his unseen audience.

Uncle Matt watched him in amazement. "You sure are a big help to me," he said. "But do you have to be so noisy about it?"

Steve explained don Luís's theory and added, "If I can bring the monkeys out of the forest, I can choose the one I want to tame."

Uncle Matt shook his head. "These are wild animals. That's why my friends and I bought part of the rain forest—to keep them safe in their own habitat. Of course, I want you to be interested in the monkeys. . . ." His expression said as plain as words that he didn't want to hurt Steve's feelings, but he had to make him understand about wild creatures.

Steve didn't want to understand. "Okay," he said, but secretly he still intended to tame a monkey.

CHAPTER THREE

STEVE LIKED taking charge of the tent.
He worked hard to do everything
well and fast. When Uncle Matt came for the midday
meal, Steve nearly always had it ready. At night his
uncle came home tired from dragging logs and tim-
bers, climbing the scaffolding, and nailing boards
that had dried in a warped shape so they didn't fit
straight. Steve made sure he had a cool supper and
a clean tent waiting. Uncle Matt talked about the
house and the pony, Ghost, that helped with the
work. Some of the work, Uncle Matt said, was too
hard for the men and the pony. He hired teams of
oxen for that.

In turn, Steve told about his adventures with don
Luís in the forest, except he called him "Don," as if
it were his first name.

Uncle Matt corrected him with a smile. "'Don' is
a title of respect. 'Luís' is his first name. Neither you,
nor I either, would ever call him by his first name
without the title." His uncle seemed glad that the
two of them were friends. "Don Luís is wise in forest
ways. He knows more about the rain forest than

anyone else because he's lived here so long. I'm hoping that he will help teach the students who come to study at our nature center. Learn everything you can from him."

Steve hadn't thought of his friendship with the elderly man as a learning situation. They had too much fun together. He hadn't really paid attention to the leaves and seeds his friend collected, nor the roots he dug, because he was too involved planning his monkey project. He had helped don Luís spread the seeds and roots on his table to dry and string the leaves and plants up near his cook stove. Every time he stepped inside the dim, one-room house, he smelled the blended spicy, minty, flowery fragrances given off by the collection. It seemed to him just smelling the air of don Luís's house would make anybody well.

"You're doing a great job here in the tent," Uncle Matt said one night after supper. "But don't work all the time. Take off whenever you'd like. Only one thing—it's safer not to venture in the forest alone. It's too easy to lose your way."

Often Steve left his pails at the spring and went to don Luís's house. He'd gotten to know the red rooster, Rojo, who strutted around the yard looking grand. Blanca, the white hen, kept busy chasing bugs, scratching in the dirt, and occasionally laying a brown egg. To the side of the porch stood a coop don Luís had made for them. Waist high to Steve, it was mounted on four strong legs and had a wire-covered door.

Rojo and Blanca spent only the nights in their

pen, walking up steps that don Luís had whacked with his machete along the length of a tree trunk. When they hopped inside, don Luís double-latched the door and pulled away the steps. Every morning, first thing, don Luís opened the door and out flew the chickens, eager to start another day.

"You will need a container to hold your monkey," don Luís pointed out, "while you make a friend of him. Perhaps one like this."

Steve studied the coop carefully, then he and don Luís, with pencil and paper, drew plans for the monkey cage. It had to be larger and more comfortable than the chickens' cage because the monkey would live in it all the time. They figured Steve would need wire fencing and boards, which he could probably get at the new house, along with a few nails.

Don Luís had an old hammer and a rusty saw he offered Steve. They oiled the saw and sharpened it, getting ready for when they'd have lumber to use it on. They spent much time discussing how to trap the monkey and what kind of bait to use. Some of their ideas were pretty wild, and they laughed a great deal.

Once, when the house-building crew took a holiday, Uncle Matt suggested to Steve that they clear a path to a river pool he knew about. "Then we could take a swim after lunch when the sun's too hot to work. Would you like that?"

"Sure." What a dandy chance to find some monkeys, maybe the big black howlers don Luís had told him about. They stayed deeper in the forest and seldom came near human beings. Here was a chance, too, to use a machete. He begged his uncle to teach him how to handle the big swordlike knife. It looked so easy when don Luís swung it. However, no matter how hard Steve tried, he couldn't get the hang of it. The machete was just too heavy and awkward. He gave it back to Uncle Matt, wiped the sweat from his face, and used a clipper to cut the head-high grass and brush.

They slashed and chopped until they cleared a narrow trail through the tangled undergrowth. Steve was steaming by the time they reached their goal, a quiet stretch of clear water long enough for swimming laps, yet not too deep for Steve's feet to touch bottom. They threw down their tools, stripped off their tee shirts, and plunged in. The cool, buoyant water made Steve feel like a joyful fish. He wagged his hands like fins and locked his feet together to

flick them from side to side like a tail. He picked a white pebble from the bottom. He rolled over and under and zigzagged between clumps of purple and white flowers floating past. He paused to look at them and smell their sweetness.

"Would my mother ever like those!" he exclaimed. "What are they?"

"Orchids. The monkeys break them off the trees."

Steve glanced up. A big black monkey was swinging, not very high, away from the river.

"A howler, I'll bet," he said, excited. "Yo! I'm here! Come back!"

The monkey jerked to a halt and looked over its shoulder. Steve waved. "Here!" To his delight, the big animal came back to a limb above the pool.

"I'm Steve from the U.S.A.," he announced, moving nearer.

The monkey stood on all fours, its tail wrapped around a higher branch. They stared at each other. Steve was surprised to see that its fur was not solid black, but light around the face, shading to a brownish beard, then to black on the remainder of its stout body. What neat flat ears! Steve wrinkled his nose, trying to catch a waft of monkey odor. No, no odor, and the monkey looked shining clean. With its intelligent eyes intently fastened on Steve's face, the howler looked ready to speak.

Steve tried some Spanish he had learned from don Luís. "You are *muy grande,* señor Howler."

Now the howler opened its mouth as if making ready to reply. Steve waited, holding his breath. The howler yawned. Its mouth gaped so wide Steve could see rows of businesslike teeth with fangs on each side.

"Hey, he's got more teeth than I do—and they're better looking!" Steve exclaimed. The monkey seemed deep in thought, staring at Steve directly below. Then it reached over to snap off a limb. Deliberately, it dropped the limb on Steve. He dodged and suffered only a glancing blow. Then the howler turned and continued on its way, traveling at a dignified pace.

"Do you think he was angry?" Steve asked, watching it disappear.

"No," said Uncle Matt. "He probably wanted to understand what you are. Or get a reaction from you."

For days Steve puzzled over the howler's behavior. What should he have done to show he wanted to be friends? He liked the big howler—maybe that would be the monkey he'd choose. He'd better collect more materials for the cage, he decided, and plan to build it larger and stronger, just in case. . . .

He was careful not to let Uncle Matt suspect what he was doing on don Luís's porch. Steve convinced himself that after he'd tamed his pet, Uncle Matt would see that he could make his monkey happy. It would be like a dog—no, like a little man that would fetch and carry for him and help him with his chores. He couldn't wait!

Early mornings when the howlers awakened him, Steve lay gently swaying in his hammock. He slept on a soft pillow stuffed with fluff from the kapok trees in their forest. Don Luís had helped him make it. Just as Uncle Matt predicted, he had come to like

the hammock better than a bed and did not get out of it until he had to. After the howlers quieted down, busy somewhere with breakfast, Steve listened for Rojo to crow, calling don Luís to open the coop and let them start their day. Soon Uncle Matt would be up and calling him. Steve grinned in anticipation of another day in the rain forest.

CHAPTER FOUR

DAY AFTER DAY Steve busied himself outside hoping monkeys would appear according to don Luís's theory. No monkeys came. He had decided the plan wouldn't work after all when Uncle Matt asked him to bathe Ghost, the hard working pony. He almost said no until his uncle added, "This time of year, the dust is so thick, Ghost is pretty miserable. He sweats as he works, then the dust coats him. He looks like he's been dipped in melted chocolate."

Steve laughed and agreed he'd do it. Uncle Matt rode the little horse back to the tent after work on Saturday because nobody worked at the house on Sundays. Steve helped tether him near their hammocks. During the night, Steve liked hearing Ghost munching grass, sighing, and blowing his lips. The next morning, with Uncle Matt at the tent to help do the chores, Steve was soon ready to gather the bath equipment—brushes made of coconut husks, a bar of soap, and buckets. He led the little brown horse to the clearing at the spring, where he tied him to a tree and set to work. Shortly after they arrived, don Luís joined them. He showed Steve how to hold onto the smooth side of the coconut husks with both hands and use the bristly side to scrub the horse into a lump of chocolate-colored soapsuds.

The dust-encrusted horse sighed with contentment and closed his eyes. For the rinse cycle, Steve doused him with buckets full of clear water from the spring. He became more and more amazed as the bath progressed—right before his eyes Ghost was turning into a white horse to match his name! Steve was so engrossed with the transformation that he didn't notice what else was happening around him till he heard don Luís call, *"Mire!* Look!"

Monkeys! Dozens of them crowded the trees around the clearing. Bright-eyed monkeys gesturing and chattering to each other as if discussing what they saw. Wow! Steve pretended he hadn't noticed them, not wanting to frighten them away, though he kept stealing glances over the horse's back. He took a long time rubbing down Ghost's shining white coat just to keep the monkeys from leaving. He felt elated, laughing with don Luís over the success of their plot.

After that, every Sunday Steve bathed Ghost, who had turned brown again after a week of work in the dust at the new house. Don Luís always came to watch the fun. Without fail the monkeys flocked down from the treetops to take ringside seats. One in particular came very near, swinging from a limb by his tail and one hand and chattering.

"He is like you, full of questions," don Luís said. Steve made-believe he knew what the monkey was asking and carefully explained everything he did during the little horse's bath. Sometimes the monkey would drop to the ground and stand on two feet like a miniature man, but he kept a safe distance away from Steve.

Squirrel monkeys, don Luís called them. They were smaller than the howlers and moved faster. Steve wondered at their name. Their quick movements were squirrel-like, and they wore russet coats, but otherwise they looked nothing like the squirrels he knew. They had a white area around their eyes, almost like a mask, and their nose and mouth were centered in a big black spot like a bull's-eye. Steve was so pleased with them, he couldn't help smiling. Now he had met the howlers and the squirrel monkeys. Maybe soon he'd meet the third kind of monkey that lived in their forest.

Don Luís suggested that the simplest trap to use for catching a monkey was a sturdy box. Steve believed he could find a suitable one in the tent if he searched long enough.

"We turn it upside down," don Luís said. "Prop up one end with a stick. Inside we have monkey bait—a thing that monkeys cannot resist. To the stick is a rope tied, like this, see?"

Suddenly, Steve understood. "Then I take the end of the rope and hide where I can watch," he exclaimed. "When a monkey goes in the box to take a look, I jerk the rope, the stick comes out, the box falls down, and we've got him! Oh, what if two go in at once? Wouldn't that be funny!" He and don Luís laughed and laughed.

They couldn't decide what bait would be best to use. It had to be a food that monkeys liked to eat, but it must not be one they could find easily in the forest. Otherwise no monkey would come to the trap. They discussed their plans every day, making changes whenever one of them had a better idea. What happy times these were for Steve! His dream of getting a pet monkey became more and more real to him.

All the while they got the tools in shape and made their plans, don Luís's two chickens scurried about the yard. Steve liked to watch Rojo find a bug and loudly call Blanca to eat it. He could see that they were pets to don Luís the way his monkey would be to him.

"Why do you shut in Blanca and Rojo at night?" Steve wondered one afternoon as he studied how the coop was made.

"I will show you." Don Luís bent over, searching in the dust. *"Mire,"* he said, pointing to a distinct paw print. It was as big as Steve's hand, with four large pads around a central pad and no claws showing. Steve squatted to examine the track while don Luís told him about the cat, *el manigordo,* that came out of the forest at night, hungry for a plump chicken. Smaller than a jaguar, the animal's big round feet gave it the name *el manigordo,* "Fat Foot."

Steve glanced toward the thick trees. "Does it eat monkeys too?"

"Sí," don Luís said. "Monkey meat tastes as *delicioso* to *el manigordo* as chicken."

Steve didn't like to hear that. For the first time he

realized the monkeys were in danger from other forest animals. How did they keep safe while they slept in the trees? Did they post a guard? More and more he wished for a library where he could find the answers to some of his questions. And he determined to make the monkey cage strong enough to protect his pet from old "Fat Foot."

CHAPTER FIVE

OCCASIONALLY, on their morning
jaunts, Steve and don Luís de-
toured by the building site. Uncle Matt was always
glad to see them, and the workers joked with don
Luís, but they kept on working. That left Steve and
his friend free to browse around and pick up scraps
of anything that might be useful in making the cage.

Steve liked to see how the house was growing.
It was a small structure, with dormitory-style bed-
rooms for students, on top of a hill that overlooked a
blue body of water Uncle Matt called the *Golfo Dulce*.
Beyond the *Golfo Dulce* to the west lay the Pacific
Ocean, he said. Everywhere else, as far as Steve's gaze
could reach, was forest—a sea of green with sometimes a taller tree rising above the rest.

Don Luís turned in every direction, as if he could
never get enough of looking. Then he said, "At your
school, do they teach the mistake that the earth is
round like a sweet orange?"

"Of course," Steve said. "Everybody knows the
earth is round."

"No, it is not true," don Luís said solemnly.

"I will show you. There is the *Golfo Dulce,* where the fishermen go. There," and he pointed north, "is where my nephew Tomás lives with his oxen. My bean field is that way." Then he pointed east. "There is my house near the spring." He pointed south. "I have never been that way, but I have heard another country is there. All flat, like a tortilla. Where is any roundness?"

Steve followed his friend's pointing finger. Despite the history books, he couldn't dispute the flatness of what they saw. The view from this hill included all the places don Luís had been in his life. To him it was the world. And it was flat. What harm was there in letting it remain that way?

Near the house stood a shelter for Ghost to be shut in at night. A dark brown pony belonging to one of the crew stayed outside. The reason gave Steve the shivers.

"After you bathe Ghost, and he's white, the vampire bats can find him," Uncle Matt explained. "They latch onto his neck, make a small cut with their sharp teeth, and lap up the blood. When they fly away before dawn, their feeding hole seals over with clotted blood, but I see the blood stains when I come to work. The vampires don't bother the dark pony. Now Ghost is safe in his pen."

"Would the vampires kill Ghost?" Steve asked, anxious.

"No," Uncle Matt said. "But he has to work hard, and I don't want him weakened by losing blood."

That gave Steve a great deal to think about. He

realized the coloring of the monkeys probably kept them safe from the vampires at night too.

Wherever he went he hoped to sight the third kind of monkey that lived in their forest, but he had no luck until one day when he and Uncle Matt went swimming. A troop of white-faced monkeys—capuchin, his uncle called them—collected above the pool, watching with their all-knowing eyes. They were the most comical looking ones yet, with white tufts of hair above their wrinkled foreheads and long tails spiraling down below the tree limbs. Their constant chirruping, at first businesslike, suddenly turned disagreeable, and they seemed to make a decision. They grabbed squishy yellow fruits from the trees and pelted Steve and his uncle. They laughed at first and dodged underwater to avoid the messy spattering. That made the monkeys more determined to hit them.

Finally Uncle Matt said, "Enough!" Climbing out of the pool, he stood to his full height, thrust out his chest, and began pounding it with his fists while roaring louder than a howler at sunset. To Steve's astonishment, the monkeys fled. What did Uncle Matt's chest-pounding say to them?

"It worked for Tarzan, and it works for me—that's all I know," Uncle Matt said smiling.

"Why do the white-faced dislike us? The others don't seem to," Steve puzzled.

Uncle Matt shook his head, indicating he did know the answer.

"Well, I don't like them either," Steve deci

"They look super smart, sort of wrinkled and bushy-headed like Albert Einstein, but they act mean."

Uncle Matt said seriously, "You're making a mistake, Steve, to think of monkeys as humans. Monkeys aren't good or bad or mean the way you're thinking. They're animals, and they act like animals."

Steve hardly heard him. The squirrel and howler monkeys appealed to him, but the white-faced didn't because they were mean. Now he wanted to meet the monkey don Luís said no longer lived in this forest, the spider monkey. Don Luís also said, besides being a tasty meal, the spider monkey was a *"muy buen leaper."* Steve hoped to find one somewhere, maybe in another part of the forest. If only he could go search!

CHAPTER SIX

THE NEXT TIME Steve went to the river pool alone, something happened that reinforced his feeling against the capuchins, and that even made him doubt the squirrel monkeys. At first he had the pool to himself—no orchids, no monkey audience to perform for, just the cool water that made him feel so refreshed. Afterward, he stretched out on a big rock to dry. The warm rock and the murmuring river made him drowsy.

Suddenly, far away but moving closer, he heard frantic squealing in the treetops. He sprang up to see a troop of terrified squirrel monkeys speeding toward him. Close behind, in fierce pursuit, came the larger capuchins. The smaller monkeys, desperate to escape to the other side of the river, leaped onto a limb above Steve. They hurled themselves across the water, arms and legs straining forward to grab hold of the nearest foliage. All but three of the squirrel monkeys had crossed safely when the capuchins caught up. Those three, with tremendous leaps, cleared the river and scrambled to what Steve thought was safety on a slender limb. He was silently cheering for them when, for no reason he could see, two of the squirrel monkeys attacked the third. They sank their teeth into it and clawed it viciously. It seemed as though they wanted to throw the other monkey to the enemies to save themselves.

Screaming in surprise, the victim fought back gamely, holding onto the limb with all four feet. Then the attackers succeeded in tearing loose its hind legs from the tree limb, and the bleeding monkey dangled, holding on desperately with its two front feet. One foot slipped, then the other, and the beaten monkey plummeted down, down, belly flopping into the swimming pool. It floated motionless while Steve, paralyzed with astonishment, watched.

He was dimly aware of the two fighters leaving the scene of the crime, swiftly following their troop. The fallen monkey looked dead, but suddenly it galvanized into a frantic dog paddle and headed for shore. Dragging its torn and bleeding body onto the rocks near Steve, it collapsed. The tragic face looked like that of a feeble old man who had been robbed and beaten by people he trusted.

Steve jumped into action, his heart pounding with excitement. Here was a monkey for taming, a monkey that needed rescuing. If only it didn't die! CPR! He racked his brain to remember what they'd learned in school about reviving people. He knew he had to turn the creature on its back and put his left hand under its neck to tilt its head. Next he'd have to pinch shut the nose—gently, like a baby's—while covering its mouth with his own. Four quick breaths— or was it five?

In his haste, he stumbled on a rock. The clatter sounded loud in the forest silence. Up shot the monkey's head. Wildly, it looked at Steve as if he were a great white giant descending upon it, an ogre more terrible than the enemy monkeys. Its eyes nearly popped out of its wrinkled face. With a scream of pure terror, more agonizing than when its friends attacked, the monkey gathered its beaten, sopping-wet body into a desperate leap for the nearest vine. Up it scrambled pell-mell to the first tree limb. From there it swung off across the river and vanished.

The capuchins, sitting quiet in the trees above Steve, witnessed everything. For some reason— maybe because their territory didn't extend beyond the river—they made no attempt to follow the small monkeys and turned their attention to Steve. Grabbing rotten sticks from around them, they hurled them down, like a steady bombardment of wet sponges.

Steve was too stricken to care. He crumpled to the rocks, sadder than he'd ever been in his life. Not because the monkey had escaped him; not because he had lost his chance for a pet; but because of that terrified look and that piercing scream, which cut right through his heart. If only the wounded monkey had known how he would have loved and cared for it! He buried his face in his arms and cried. Not a simple straightforward kind of crying the way his sister cried, but wrenching, body-shaking sobs that took hold of him and wouldn't let go.

He never remembered crying in his whole life. He never cared enough about anything to cry over it.

But now it was as if a tornado had hold of him and wouldn't let go. He thrashed about in the ferns, beat the ground with his fists, and kicked in frustration and sorrow.

Finally, all cried out, he rolled over and looked around. The capuchins had gone. Their rotted sticks lay scattered about him. The forest steamed silently in the hot afternoon sun. He smelled the warm cinnamon odor of the ferns he'd smashed. Breathing a long shuddering sigh, he reached for his shirt to wipe his nose. For a while, sitting there, he wished to be again the old Steve who stood on the sidelines and minded his own business—the Steve who never got involved in anything, who never cried a tear, and who never had his feelings hurt.

Then he shook himself, knowing that he could not go back to being that boy again, even if he wanted to. And maybe he didn't really want to.

Slowly, like a person who'd been sick a long time, he crawled into the pool to wash off the sand and bathe his hot face. Trudging back to the tent along the narrow trail, he did some heavy thinking. He could not give up the plan to tame a monkey. But now he knew it would be hard work. He definitely decided against a capuchin. Maybe he didn't want a squirrel monkey either—look how treacherous those two friends had been. Maybe the big, bearded howler should be his choice, even though it raised a rumpus that could be heard for miles. The neighbors back home would be sure to complain. He needed to talk to don Luís about it. Then they would decide.

CHAPTER SEVEN

ON ONE of their scouting trips, don
Luís pointed out a tree hanging
with green beans almost two feet long. A *guabo* tree,
he explained. Using the machete, he slashed off a
pod and split it. Inside was something that looked
like fluffy cotton candy. Nested in the fluff were large
beans, which he demonstrated should be popped in
the mouth, not for eating, but for using the tongue
and teeth to remove the cotton, spitting out the
bean afterward. That seemed odd at first, until Steve
tasted how delicious the fluff was—better than cotton candy at the state fair.

"Yummmmm," he murmured, too busy pulling
the heavy pods to talk. They ate the sweet filling
from several, and Steve brought one to the tent for
Uncle Matt to sample.

"That's good!" his uncle exclaimed. "Let's go for
more."

Steve emptied the morning's harvest from his
string bag, and they headed for the *guabo* tree. Too
late! Squirrel monkeys perched on every limb, holding on with their tails while they split green pods,

lifted out the cotton candy to cram in their mouths, and discarded the remainder. Empty green shells littered the ground under the tree.

Uncle Matt laughed at the sight. "Next time let's come early to get our share," was all he said.

The monkeys proved don Luís right again. They hadn't discovered the *guabo* tree until they spied Steve and don Luís enjoying the sweet fluff. Then they must have sent the news throughout the forest, before Uncle Matt and Steve could return.

"How could they get here so fast?" Steve wondered.

Don Luís showed him the reason—"monkey ladder" vines that he called *escalera de mono*. They grew everywhere, even into the tops of the tallest trees and beyond to other trees. Monkeys used them for roadways through the tree tops, don Luís said. At eye level, some of the vines were as wide as Steve's body.

He liked the rolling sound of *escalera de mono*. He thought of the words as meaning "monkey escalator" and used them whenever he could in his conversation. And he conversed often now because he had so much to talk about and there was so much he wanted to know. He had learned that people couldn't give him all the answers he needed. Books! He wished for a whole library of books about monkeys so he could understand what he observed about them. He had never given any thought to what he'd be when he grew up, but now he was certain he wanted to study monkeys. He didn't know what a monkey specialist was called, but he intended to find out.

Steve had learned that the forest was filled with many different kinds of surprises. Once on a gathering expedition they came to the edge of a clearing beside the river, a place Steve had never seen before. Don Luís hesitated, as if he hadn't intended to come here. He half turned away, hesitated again, and seemed to change his mind. Putting a finger against his lips, he made Steve understand that here was a secret. Then he led the way into the clearing.

Steve gasped. Great round stones stood in rows, many stones in many rows. Some of them were higher than don Luís's head and as massive as bull elephants. Others were smaller. All of them were gray and ancient. He wanted to reach out and touch one, but he dared not. These enormous stones had to be man-made and had to have been arranged in

these rows by human beings. How could mere humans have done it? An eerie feeling crept over him, as if he stood in a deserted cathedral. Don Luís, he saw, felt awed too.

Steve whispered, "What are these?"

Don Luís shook his head. "A long time they have stood here. Nobody remembers when they came. . . ." His voice trailed away. He spoke as if the stones had life in them, had minds of their own. Steve shivered though the warm, humid air pressed against him from all sides.

Around some of the stone spheres, the bare earth was pitted as if an upheaval had taken place.

"What happened?" Steve indicated the torn up earth.

"Los huaqueros," don Luís said in a low voice. "Treasure seekers."

Steve repeated, *"Los huaqueros?"* Who would come seeking treasure? The people in the forest lived plainly. Nobody was wealthy. Where would any treasure be?

Don Luís could see Steve puzzling over the word, so he attempted another explanation. "Grave robbers."

"Grave robbers?" Now Steve was really shocked. "That doesn't make any sense to me." He and don Luís exchanged words in Spanish and English but couldn't understand each other.

Later, Steve asked Uncle Matt what he knew about treasure seekers, grave robbers, and *huaqueros.* "I don't believe don Luís can be right that they're all the same."

"He is right," Uncle Matt assured him. "But *hua-queros* are illegal now. Laws have been passed forbidding them."

"I can see why grave robbing would be against the law," Steve argued, "but what's wrong with treasure hunting? Besides, what treasure is there to hunt?"

"There used to be lots of treasure—gold, jade, pottery—some of it very fine. Centuries ago, these treasures were placed in tombs when an important person like a chief died. *Huaqueros* break into these graves and steal the valuables."

Then Steve decided to tell about the enormous, perfectly round stones that don Luís had said must be kept secret. He knew that Uncle Matt could be trusted, and he wanted desperately to learn more about them.

His uncle listened with interest. "I've heard they were here somewhere, but I didn't know if it was true," he said. "Some ancient civilization shaped them. How or why, nobody knows. *Huaqueros* are always looking for stone spheres and for the graves that are sometimes nearby."

No wonder Steve got the chills when he stood among those strange stones!

"I wish I could find some of those treasures!" he said, thinking out loud. "I'd sell 'em and buy a monkey."

"You wouldn't if you understood." Uncle Matt's voice was low and sad. "When the *huaqueros* break into a grave to take what they call 'treasures,' they destroy other things that are priceless too, things that would tell us the reason for those stones, why they're arranged that way, and how those people had the know-how to shape them and to transport them. Now we may never find out."

Steve's curiosity about the stone spheres grew the more he thought about them. He liked the name Uncle Matt had for them, "the Enigmas." He wanted to return to that mysterious place by the river, but don Luís wouldn't talk about going back, and Steve realized he could never find the way by himself.

He realized, too, how right Uncle Matt was to condemn the *huaqueros*. He burned with anger himself because he so much wanted an explanation for those humongous spheres, chiseled with precision, and the *huaqueros* destroyed the clues. Over and over he turned round in his mind the questions: Where did the Enigmas come from? He had never seen rocks like them in this area. Who made such perfect spheres out of them, and how did they do it? How did the makers transport them here? And, most of all, why? What purpose did they serve?

If he could go back to the Enigmas, he'd search for the graves that might be nearby. Hundreds, maybe thousands, of years old! He shivered, partly from fear, partly from excitement. He wanted to go back, though he knew now that he would never dig in a place sacred to don Luís, not even to find an artifact that could be sold or traded for a monkey.

CHAPTER EIGHT

ON A BRIGHT, clear day when Steve went for water, he found don Luís talking to a stranger at the spring. The stranger spoke English and introduced himself as Ron, a botanist who was studying plants in the rain forest.

"My plant press," he said, gesturing toward an awkward looking bundle on the ground beside his backpack. "I collect leaves of plants I don't know and press them in there. When I go back to the university, I study them."

He looked as if he'd been in the forest a long time in his bleached jeans, worn thin at the knees, and his scuffed and scratched boots. His machete, hanging from a belt instead of a rope like don Luís's, caught Steve's attention. It was sheathed in a fine leather holster that was decorated like a cowboy's fancy saddle. A small matching holster held his sharpening file.

Ron dipped his cupped hands in the spring and drank. He then wiped his wet hands over his face and shoved his hat to the back of his sun-bleached hair. "I thought I'd look around in this area for a while, sort of prospecting for unknown plants, so to speak. Do you know anything about using plants to help sick people or sick animals?"

"*Sí,*" don Luís said. "Many plants are helpful. You stay at my house. Look all you want. I teach you about plants."

Steve left his buckets at the spring while he went with the others to don Luís's small house. There they moved aside the monkey cage supplies and settled Ron's backpack in the cleared space. They strung his hammock between two of the posts that held up the porch roof. Now he was, as Ron laughingly said, in residence at the inn of don Luís.

After that, they roved the forest together, the two men with their machetes swinging from their waists, and Steve carrying the plant press. What his elderly friend knew about nature remedies fascinated Steve even more than the fruits don Luís had already taught him. One of the strangest was the snake bite tree. It had egg-shaped seed pods and one huge seed inside an orange, leathery skin.

"Man, that would cure you or kill you," Ron said. "With the fer-de-lances showing up where you least expect them, I'm sure glad to know about it."

Of all the plants don Luís showed them, Steve thought the cow tree had to be the most useful. When his friend pierced the tree's bark with his machete, out flowed a milklike liquid. "See? Always food is here. Much *la leche.*" He showed them how to catch the milk in their mouths. It tasted good to Steve. "It will cure sickness of the stomach." He peeled off a section of the bark. "Drown the skin in water many hours. Beat." He picked up a rock and pounded the ground to demonstrate. "Then you make a *cobija*—a cover." He moved his arms, as if wrapping a blanket around himself.

He went on to explain how the long-ago people used what the forest gave them. They had no way to go to the town to buy medicines or visit a doctor. "People yet use the plants," he said.

"That's why I want to learn about them," Ron said. "So I can help people get well."

Ron took the bark and the leaves he collected, spread them carefully in the plant press, then strapped the layers of the wooden press tightly together while they dried. He collected seeds and labeled them and made many notes in a small book he carried in his pocket.

Whenever they needed bananas, don Luís cut a bunch with his machete, and the two men hauled it to the porch where they hung it from the rafters. All of them took fruit from the bunch as it ripened. The supply never ran out, and no wonder—Steve counted sixty-eight bananas in one bunch. He didn't know bananas could taste so delicious. He and Uncle Matt invented a recipe that was the best! They fried very ripe bananas in a black-iron skillet with a little oil for breakfast. Ron preferred to eat them right from the bunch, while don Luís turned them into a jam.

Ron seemed to be interested in everything. He was intrigued with the monkey cage and the plans to capture a monkey. "I'll help you," he said enthusiastically. "But it won't be easy to catch one. They can move through the trees at forty miles an hour, you know. That's fast traveling!"

Steve agreed, impressed, and don Luís nodded wisely.

While they hammered together the boxy frame they'd sawed from the lumber scraps, they swapped monkey stories. Steve told about what happened at the swimming pool that day when the capuchins chased the squirrel monkeys, and a squirrel monkey was betrayed by its friends. The others had no explanation, though Ron promised to see if he could find out the reason when he returned to school.

Every day was more exciting with Ron around. He knew many things that Steve had wanted to find out. He showed Ron a tree growing not far from the spring. It was loaded with pale-green flowers that smelled sweeter than anything Steve had ever known before. The air around the spring was so heavy with the cloying sweetness that Steve sometimes thought the water tasted like it. Ron called it an ylang-ylang tree, and spelled it for him. "No wonder you like to smell it," he added. "The flowers are used to make expensive perfumes."

Sometimes Ron went away, hiking to meet the bus that passed on the Pan-American highway. Other times, he vanished into the rain forest. Always he came back with new stories to tell. Steve liked best the one about the monkey mother Ron saw leaping from one tree to another with her baby riding piggyback, its front paws clutching her fur, its tail curled around the base of her tail. What a fun ride, sailing through the air, safe on its mother's back! Hearing about sights like that made Steve want more than ever to go deep into the forest.

The squirrel monkeys continued to be spectators at Ghost's Sunday baths. Steve grew more and more fond of the monkey that walked around like a little man. Not only was he inquisitive about everything, but he put on a show, knowing that Steve, don Luís, and Ron admired him.

"What a clown," said Ron, watching him swing from limb to limb, then hang upside down, looking at them to make sure he had their attention. Then he twirled round and round till Steve's head spun.

"Clown! The exact, right name for him," Steve said, laughing.

CHAPTER NINE

AFTER TWO MONTHS in the rain forest, food supplies ran low, and the carpenters needed more building materials for the house.

"We'll have to make a trip to Los Cocos," Uncle Matt said, getting a sheet of paper and a pencil. Together they made a long list of things to buy and errands to run.

"Don't you want to write your folks and let them know how you are?" Uncle Matt asked. "We'll be going to the post office to pick up mail tomorrow."

Steve meant to write at least a note, but he ran out of time because they went to bed early. And anyway, he saw that Uncle Matt had written them a long letter. The next morning they hurriedly ate breakfast by lantern light. Just before going out to the truck, Steve slipped a banana into his pocket in case he needed a midmorning snack.

The old truck started reluctantly, and off they went. Steve tried not to miss any of the scenery while the truck jounced over the washed-out road. It was the roughest ride he'd ever taken. What with the heat in the cab—it was hot as a popcorn popper—and the grinding jolts, he felt like a kernel of corn exploding in every direction.

The truck overheated, spewing steam from the radiator, and then a tire blew out.

"We'll be late getting there," Uncle Matt said as they hurried to patch the tire and force air into it with a hand pump. "We'll have to rush with our errands so we can start home before dark."

When they finally pulled into town and parked, Steve checked his teeth to make sure none of them had shaken loose. He looked with curiosity at the shops and offices lining both sides of the narrow main street, which was only about three blocks long. No one was in sight as he jumped down from the truck.

"The middle of the day—everybody's eating," Uncle Matt explained. "But the lumber yard might be open."

Steve had turned to follow him when a strange thing appeared some distance away on the deserted street. He stopped short. "L-l-look!" he stuttered, pointing toward a small upright dog coming toward them at a staggering run. It clutched a large box tight against its chest, and a long tail trailed behind. Close on the creature's heels ran a red-faced woman with a folded newspaper upraised like a club. She screeched a jumble of Spanish and English, which Steve heard clearly but couldn't understand. What he did understand was that she wanted to catch the thing she was chasing.

Out of an alley behind the woman appeared a

rumpled man, also running. "Stop him!" he yelled. "Matt! Stop that monkey!"

"It's the Smalleys, from the jungle," Uncle Matt exclaimed. "Come on! Let's help!"

"Help with what?" Steve shouted, charging after his uncle. His heart had leaped when he heard the magic word "monkey." He had never imagined he would find a monkey in town! Here they were racing head-on to meet one, but the monkey saw them coming and ducked into another alley.

Now more people appeared in the monkey's wake. One was a pretty young woman, black hair fanning out behind her, necklaces and bracelets glittering against her black dress. Steve wondered how she could run in those high heels. "Eduardo," she gasped as she passed them.

"He stole the eggs!" cried a plump man in a tie and dark suit following her. Behind him panted an older man, his white shirt and trousers matching his hair. He was so out of breath he could only raise a hand in greeting.

Uncle Matt and Steve were fresh. They joined the chase, Uncle Matt in the lead with the angry Mrs. Smalley. Steve took up a rear position beside the puffing man in white. From there he could see everyone and also glimpse the fleeing monkey out front. What did Ron say about monkey speed? Forty miles per hour! Steve believed it. We'll never catch him, he thought. Soon he was breathing as hard as his running partner.

"Don't let him reach the trees!" Mr. Smalley shouted ahead. "He'll get away for sure."

The *señorita* in high heels forged past Mrs. Smalley, then Uncle Matt passed them both. Steve gathered his strength and shot forward in time to see the monkey duck into an abandoned warehouse. He entered the cavernous building with Uncle Matt and the *señorita*, only seconds behind Eduardo. Even so, the monkey had vanished among the piles of debris.

Frantically the *señorita* said, "We MUST find him before Mrs. Smalley comes. She will beat him, she is so angry." She plowed right in, upturning boxes, flinging old newspapers and trash right and left.

Out of breath as he was, Steve still managed to dive in beside her. Uncle Matt searched not far away, a determined set to his jaw. Steve knew he meant to find Mrs. Smalley's eggs, whereas the *señorita* and Steve meant to find Eduardo.

Already Steve was thinking of this monkey by his name, as if he knew him personally. He'd do anything to prevent a beating for Eduardo. More than that, he wanted to see Eduardo close-up and touch him. He wanted Eduardo to look at him, Steve, and recognize him as a friend.

The others clattered in at the far door, Mrs. Smalley's indignant voice echoing against the ceiling. Steve redoubled his efforts, coughing from the clouds of dust he and the *señorita* raised.

Now they uncovered a big box, far back in the corner. "I think he's here," she whispered. "See this hole? It's just his size. Careful now." They slowly pulled open a flap, and there sat the little monkey clutching a box labeled *Huevos Frescos*. He looked at the *señorita* as if he expected a scolding. But she greeted him in Spanish, calling him by his name as she reached toward him with her sparkling bracelets jingling. In English she said to Steve, "When he is distracted, gently take the box away."

Eduardo stared at all the pretty bracelets. She slid them along her arm toward him and made them tinkle and chime. The monkey's intelligent brown eyes focused on the jewelry. He shifted his feet and leaned forward. Steve braced himself, ready to do as she had asked him.

Hesitatingly, Eduardo reached out his left hand, still holding fast to the box with his right hand and his tail. As he touched one of the dangling charms, and the *señorita* continued talking softly in Spanish, Steve took hold of the box and tugged. Eduardo slowly relaxed his grip without noticing what was happening. He reached both hands toward the jewelry. Steve could not resist—before backing away, he stroked the monkey's soft fur, something he thought he'd never have a chance to do. Now he remembered the banana he had brought along for a snack. Moving in slow motion, he slipped it out of his pocket. At least Eduardo would have something to replace the eggs.

He showed the fruit to the monkey's friend. She smiled and shaped "Okay" with her mouth. Keeping Eduardo's attention on the bracelets, she took the banana with her other hand. Placing it on top of her braceleted arm, she held it out to him. Right away, Eduardo accepted the fruit. He inspected it before breaking the peel and raising the ivory-colored banana to his mouth. The *señorita* and Steve inched away backward and joined the others still searching at the far end of the shed.

"My eggs!" Mrs. Smalley shrieked, clambering over boxes toward Steve. "We haven't had eggs at our house for a month. No way was that monkey going to get away with these!" She flipped up the box lid. Not an egg was broken. Satisfied, the chasers filed out of the old building, wiping their sweaty faces with their handkerchiefs and straightening their disarrayed clothes. That is, everyone except the *señorita,* who looked as if she'd never left her cool office. Steve gave a last backward glance, wishing he could watch Eduardo eat the banana.

As the group walked down the street, the Smalleys pieced together the story of what had happened. "That Eduardo is a pest," Mrs. Smalley said. "I know it isn't his fault—he was somebody's pet until he became too troublesome. Then they threw him out. Now he has no home. . . ." She paused to catch her breath.

"Begs and steals for a living," Mr. Smalley contributed, smoothing his hair.

It all started at their lawyer's office—Mrs. Smalley gestured toward the man in the suit, who inclined his head and smiled at Steve and Uncle Matt. "We were signing some papers, in a hurry to leave for home. Everything we'd bought today piled around us—"

"In through the window popped Eduardo," her husband interrupted. "Grabbed the first thing he came to—the egg box—and scooted out again."

That's when everybody leaped to the chase—both

of the Smalleys; their lawyer; his secretary, the young woman in black; his clerk, the white-haired gentleman; and later on, Steve and Uncle Matt. Seven people after one small monkey! Steve hid a grin with his hand. He had a feeling the monkey won.

Before the chasers separated at the lawyer's office, amid thank-yous from the Smalleys, Steve managed to ask a question that had been on the tip of his tongue ever since seeing that small figure running toward him.

"What kind of monkey is Eduardo?" He held his breath waiting for the answer.

It was the secretary who smiled at him and gave him the answer he hoped for: "Why, spider monkey, of course." Her name was señorita Dahlia Moreno, and Steve thought it as pretty as she was.

CHAPTER TEN

FOR THE REST of the afternoon, while
Steve hurried from the post office
to the town hall and from store to store with Uncle
Matt, his heart sang, "Eduardo, the spider monkey!
The fourth kind of monkey, the one not in our forest
now. And I touched him! I've got to see him again.
Maybe he'll come back."

Steve glanced about, hopeful, everywhere they
went, even in the hardware store, but it wasn't
Eduardo he sighted. It was a familiar tall figure, hat
brim tilted back to show his sunburned face. Ron!
He didn't see Steve, concentrating as he was on
something he held in his hand. Steve rushed over to
greet him. Ron dropped the tool on the counter—it
looked like a small shovel of some kind, but Steve
was so glad to see his friend, he didn't really notice.

Ron greeted him with a wide smile and clasped
his shoulder. "Hi, there, old pal. Am I ever glad to see
you." He looked over Steve's head. "And is this your
uncle?"

Steve introduced them. Watching the two men
shake hands, Steve could see that Ron was younger

than Uncle Matt. Maybe that was why he was friend-
lier. Uncle Matt's eyes looked quiet and reserved, as if
he were evaluating Ron in some way. Both of them
seemed in a hurry—Steve knew he and Uncle Matt
had more to do before leaving for home—so they
soon said good-bye, with Ron giving Steve's shoulder
another friendly clasp, almost like a secret signal,
and saying, "See you around!"

In the afterglow of seeing Ron so unexpectedly,
Steve almost forgot Eduardo. But by the time they
headed for the last stop, the food store, he remembered and dragged his feet in disappointment.

"Move along," Uncle Matt said, urging Steve
through the screen door. "We must get home before
dark."

Inside, light was dim because of all the items
stacked around and hanging from the ceiling. Two
or three shoppers, carrying baskets on their arms,
moved about looking at the merchandise. The store-
keeper stood at the cash register, pencil in hand to
list purchases and add up the cost. Steve noticed
what a long time that took for each customer, but
nobody seemed to mind.

Suddenly a shopper called out, "Eduardo!"
Everyone turned to look. Sure enough, the long-
legged, long-armed, long-tailed monkey pressed his
face against the screen door, peering inside. The low
afternoon sun lighted the tip ends of his hairs, out-
lining his body in silver. He really did resemble a
giant spider.

The shoppers murmured to each other,
"Eduardo," and surged toward the door. But Steve

was in front, only to see Eduardo turn and flee. He leaped to the top of the first fence he came to, a very high fence, and disappeared. Steve recalled don Luís saying the spider monkey was a *"muy buen* leaper." That was certainly true about Eduardo. He made great leaps with little effort.

Down the alley Steve ran, planning to intercept the monkey and take another look. But by then Eduardo was heading for the outskirts of town, leaping from tree to tree. Steve stood gazing after him. Everything had happened so fast he'd only gotten a glimpse of the monkey this time, but that was better than not seeing him again.

There in the dust of the street watching Eduardo fade in the distance, he felt troubled. Eduardo lived in fear; most of his life was spent running from people. Also, this second meeting with the spider monkey showed him that Eduardo looked sort of ratty, not healthy and clean like Clown and the other rain forest monkeys. What a lonely life he must lead—no troop to belong to, no relatives or friends. Begging wouldn't be a very sure way of getting food either. Probably he went to bed hungry some nights. And stealing was dangerous. Somebody could hurt Eduardo for stealing.

The more he thought of the displaced monkey, the clearer he understood what Uncle Matt meant about leaving monkeys wild—that monkeys need other monkeys, and they need their home in the rain forest. Even so, Steve could not yet give up his plan to capture a monkey of his own.

CHAPTER ELEVEN

*S*TEVE CONTINUED work on his secret project whenever he could get away from the tent. Now he pictured Eduardo occupying the cage. The town monkey had no real home. He didn't belong to anybody. Why couldn't Eduardo become his monkey? That way Steve wouldn't be kidnapping a monkey from the forest—Eduardo had already been taken out of the forest and had no family.

He often thought of other things that changed his attitude. He and don Luís had once startled a troop of howlers busily eating leaves in a tree. The troop fled, but one young monkey, unable to jump across the distance to the next tree, sat at the end of a limb and screamed for help. An older monkey, who had already disappeared to safety, came hurrying back, and what it did Steve would never forget. It clasped the tip of the branch it was on with both hind feet and made a powerful leap across the gap to the stranded youngster, still crouching at the tip end of its branch and still screaming.

The large monkey, bending the tree and pulling the branch behind it, connected with the small monkey's branch, clasping the end. The terrified screaming stopped, and the little monkey scurried across the bridge made by the big howler's body into the farther tree and vanished. Then the large monkey swung easily back the way it had come, following the youngster it had rescued.

Getting to know the joyful Clown and his troop also affected Steve's thinking. He now believed that to trap and steal a monkey would be the same as kidnapping somebody's relative—an uncle or aunt, mother or father, sister or brother, child or nephew. The monkeys seemed too human, feeling sorrow, guilt, happiness, and contentment just as Steve did. They cared a lot for each other, and they expressed themselves in a language that they understood, even though Steve didn't. He faced the fact that as much as he wanted a monkey, he couldn't steal one.

Now all depended on somehow getting Eduardo. But considering the distance Steve was from town, that seemed impossible too.

After an absence of several weeks, Ron reappeared at the spring with a big grin. He didn't refer to seeing Steve and Uncle Matt in Los Cocos, but he said, "Say, I heard about your big rescue of the town monkey— you and that pretty *señorita* from the lawyer's office. Tell me about it."

Steve told his version of the chase while Ron and don Luís, who never tired of hearing it, chuckled. Afterward Ron said, "Well, I've got some late-breaking news for you—that monkey's in real trouble now. He stole a whole chicken a woman had ready to put in the oven for her family. Everybody's saying that nothing's safe from that mischievous monkey."

Steve's heart sank. What if somebody decided to do away with Eduardo? To exile him from town, or to kill him?

"Could we bring him here to our forest?" For the first time he put into words what he'd been thinking since he saw Eduardo.

His friends were silent, as if each one waited for the other to speak.

Don Luís cleared his throat and stared at the ground. "No spider monkeys have been in this forest for twenty-five years. The monkeys that are remaining would drive him out—or worse. Much worse."

"Most of his life he's been a town monkey, begging and stealing," Ron added. "He couldn't survive in the wild."

"I'll teach him! He's smart—he'll learn!"

In his heart, Steve knew that what they said was true, but he felt he had to save the town monkey in spite of their arguments.

The days passed quickly. Time for another trip to Los Cocos, and Steve wasn't ready. He hastily wrote a letter to his parents by lantern light the night before. The next day as he entered the post office, he saw a strange boy reflected in the glass of the door, a boy who appeared taller and who had no bulges showing under his tee shirt. He was so surprised and pleased, he went through the door twice just to double-check. Could that be the same person his dresser mirror at home used to reflect? He could hardly believe it!

He decided to send a postcard to his sister—he hadn't forgotten what she'd called him—and on it he scrawled, "You can't call me a couch potato now!" Let her think that over! Then he scribbled a line on another card for his grandparents. He chose pictures of monkeys, and he picked the prettiest postage stamps to paste on the cards.

As usual, Uncle Matt had many errands to do. Steve tagged along to carry bundles, keeping alert for sight of Eduardo. All day he saw no sign of him. They came to the food store, their last stop. Still, no Eduardo. He dared not ask any of the shopkeepers about him. He didn't know who might be the monkey's enemy. Suddenly, he thought of someone who for sure was Eduardo's friend—the pretty *señorita*. He very well remembered where the lawyer's office was located.

Taking a deep breath, he said to Uncle Matt, "While you finish here, I'll run to the truck with these packages. That way it'll be easier to handle the groceries." Without waiting for his surprised uncle to answer, he bolted for the door. The lawyer's office was a little way beyond where the truck was parked in the shade. He threw the bundles inside, not bothering to lock the door—nobody ever did—and loped to see the *señorita*, hoping she'd be in.

She was, and she recognized Steve right away. He didn't have time to greet her politely, as people did here. Breathlessly, he explained why he'd come. "How is Eduardo?"

She admitted the monkey committed a prank with serious consequences but assured Steve that for the present he was all right. "Eduardo is a monkey caught between two worlds," she said. "He doesn't belong anywhere."

In a tumble of words, Steve confided to her his plan to make Eduardo his own. He told her how he and his friends were building a fine, roomy cage for him and how much he wanted the monkey. "He won't ever have to be afraid again," Steve promised. "He'll always have good food, and I'll look out for him." He saw the doubt spreading over her face, so he repeated how well he'd take care of Eduardo.

She laid her hand on his arm and said softly, "I'm sure you would, but it may not be wise—I don't know what to say. What about your uncle? Does he want Eduardo?"

Steve's silence answered her.

She said, "I promise you—if there's any way you can help Eduardo—if he's in real danger, I'll send you word."

"Thank you—*muchas gracias*. My uncle—once he sees how happy I'll make Eduardo—he'll be okay. I have to go."

She smiled. "*Adiós*, don Esteban."

"*Adiós*, señorita Moreno. Don't forget!" He was out the door headed for the food store in a flash, but Uncle Matt was already at the truck, packing the things they'd bought in an orderly way in the back. Steve helped arrange the overflow and the breakables in the cab. They then fitted themselves in, slammed the doors hard, and rumbled off toward home.

CHAPTER TWELVE

A T THE SPRING one afternoon, Ron sat sharpening his machete with his *lima* and waiting for Steve. "Come on over to don Luís's, and let's finish the cage," he suggested.

Steve hesitated. He wanted ever so much to go with Ron, but this afternoon he'd promised Uncle Matt he'd work in the garden. He set his buckets down, however, and followed Ron, who chatted about town and the things he'd seen.

At the house while the three of them worked on the cage and the trap, they continued talking about Eduardo, monkeys in general, and the rain forest around them.

"Where did you learn to speak English?" Ron asked don Luís.

The older man's face broke into a surprised smile. "When I was young—*un niño*—I sold to *los turistas* on *la carretera.*"

"You mean the Pan-American highway?" Ron quizzed.

"*Sí.* I sold them many things—*gasolina, aspirina, chocolate*—many things."

"Monkeys?" Steve asked.

"No monkeys," don Luís said.

"You grew up around here then?" Ron pursued his questions.

"*Sí*."

"You own this land, this house?" Ron's face was intent, his words careful.

"There is a paper. It tells this house is mine while I am alive."

"Your family was from long ago?" Ron continued.

Don Luís seemed to consider this question from all angles before answering. "*Sí*. Some of my people were of the Indians. Some were from the Spanish times."

"You must know the forest well—you have been all over this countryside?" Ron made a sweeping gesture with his arm to include the rain forest.

Steve wondered why Ron pressed don Luís for such personal information.

Don Luís said nothing.

"I've been thinking," Ron said, tilting his head and squinting his eyes to gauge the fit of the cage door. "In all this forest around here there're probably some villages from long ago. You know, maybe some old rock piles, or those big stones I've heard so much about."

Don Luís remained silent.

Steve opened his mouth, eager to tell Ron about the mysterious stone spheres that might be near a burial ground. Then he remembered—those ancient secrets belonged to don Luís. He snapped his mouth shut so fast his teeth clicked in the silence. Ron looked at him, alert. Steve looked at don Luís.

The older man merely pointed to a place on the cage door and remarked, "A nail is needed here."

Steve couldn't believe don Luís wouldn't tell their friend about so great a discovery. His hand trembled as he held a small nail where don Luís had pointed, then Ron hammered it in.

"You know, those 'stone spheres,' I think they're called." Ron spoke lightly, almost as if he were joking. "Somebody told me there used to be a bunch of them near the river here. I bet you've seen them, kid?" He made the statement a question, demanding an answer.

Steve reached for another nail, but Ron stayed his hand, encircling Steve's wrist with his thumb and forefinger. In the strained silence, Steve felt he had to get away before he said something he shouldn't. He jerked free and scrambled to his feet. "I've got to get back to the tent—gotta dig some *yuca*—er—I promised Uncle Matt. . . ."

Don Luís didn't look up. His calm face and steady fingers gave no hint that he heard anything that was being said.

Ron's eyes glittered from under his bleached eyebrows. "Yeah, kid, you'd better get back to that tent," he drawled. "Unca Matt's sure got an easy life— a servant to do all the dirty work. You run along."

Steve fled, pausing at the spring only long enough to fill the pails. At the tent, he slammed down the buckets on the table, sloshing water over the top edge. Then he rushed to the garden. Working at a furious pace doing the things he'd promised Uncle Matt, he tried to blank out the words Ron said and the way Ron had looked.

Why was Ron so angry? What had happened in those few seconds to come between three good friends? Maybe don Luís misunderstood Ron—that was why he didn't answer. But Ron had repeated the question. Then he'd said that other hateful thing. Steve winced, recalling what Ron said about Uncle

Matt. It wasn't true. Steve liked helping Uncle Matt. He liked living in the tent surrounded by the forest.

By the time he went inside to make supper, he had pushed to the back of his mind everything bad that had happened on don Luís's porch. He remembered only that the cage was nearly finished, and before long he could get his monkey.

CHAPTER THIRTEEN

SOON AFTER THAT Ron went away again, disappearing into the forest with no word as to where he was going or when he'd be back. In a way, Steve felt relieved because Ron's surliness made him uncomfortable. Thinking back, it seemed to him Ron had changed in ways he couldn't understand. Still, he missed Ron and hoped when he came back he would be his old self.

What made Ron's going away more difficult than before was that don Luís announced that he too had to go away to the farm of his nephew Tomás. There he would help with the planting of *el arroz, el melón, los frijoles.* "The planting will take many days, much work."

"When will you come back?"

"Before two months, *si Dios quiere.*" That last phrase his friend used often, especially when he planned for the future. Steve knew it meant "if God so wants." He also knew that rice and beans were the mainstay of don Luís's diet. He ate them three times a day, every day. When Blanca laid an egg, he ate a boiled egg, in addition to the fruit they gathered.

Steve realized don Luís had to make sure of his food supply, but he wished both his friends didn't have to go away at the same time.

It so happened that don Luís's departure was delayed because Blanca disappeared. It was not a case of *el manigordo*, don Luís told Steve as they searched for her. "She has not laid an egg for me in a while," he said. "I am thinking she has made a nest somewhere, and in that nest she has a collection of eggs that she is sitting on. She thinks that one day she will come out of hiding with a family of small chickens to surprise me."

"But won't *el manigordo* get her?" Steve worried.

"If he can," his friend answered. "We must find her and remove her to safety."

They looked everywhere that Blanca could have made a nest. They simply couldn't find her. Don Luís was anxious to leave for the planting before the rains began, but he would not go without finding Blanca.

The two of them sat on the old log in the shade one morning discussing what to do. Steve suggested that don Luís go, and he would continue the search. Don Luís said he couldn't without knowing if Blanca was safe. That brought them to a dead end, so they kept quiet.

In the silence, Steve heard a rustle, then a soft clucking.

He and don Luís leaped to their feet.

"She is here!" Don Luís exclaimed.

"But where?" Steve asked, bewildered. Blanca could not hide behind the log nor under it. Then Steve clapped his head. Why hadn't he thought of it? He and don Luís seemed to read each other's minds. Without a word, they moved to the end of the log, squatted down, and looked inside the hollow. There sat Blanca, her white feathers fluffed out around her as she snuggled in the leaves, dried grass, and kapok that she had shaped into a nest. Don Luís stretched his long arm into the hollow log, gently pulling Blanca, nest and all, toward them. He lifted her into his arms.

Steve counted seven warm brown eggs in the concave nest she had made. The white hen fussed and clucked and pretended to peck them. Don Luís stroked her and spoke softly in her tiny pink ear. He put Blanca inside the chicken coop, then he and Steve moved the nest and all the eggs in with her. Right away, Blanca settled down, clucking and arranging the eggs under her feathers with her beak. She made sure to cover them all.

"I don't understand," Steve said, watching her. "Why didn't *el manigordo* eat her?"

Don Luís chuckled. "Come and see. The hole in the log is too small for señor Spotted Cat. You see?" He measured the diameter of the hollow, then he stretched the length of his arm. "Also his arm is not so long as this one. He could not reach her. Blanca is wise, but not so wise as don Luís." He laughed again.

Now he made haste to leave for the farm. Steve promised to take good care of Blanca and Rojo and the baby chicks that would probably hatch while his friend was away.

"Lock the cage with care every night," instructed don Luís. *"El manigordo* will be looking for them."

"Ole Fat Foot will be disappointed—I'll see to that," Steve assured him.

Even though don Luís and Ron had left, Steve continued to work on the monkey cage. He thought up little things to do to make the cage more handsome. Using a piece of sandpaper he'd found discarded at the new house, he smoothed the rough spots and the corners. He felt content sitting alone on don Luís's porch, making Eduardo's cage strong and comfortable.

It was there that Uncle Matt found him when he came home unexpectedly from the house site. There was no time to try to hide his project—his uncle was already coming up the steps before Steve realized he was near. Guiltily, Steve stood up and faced him. Uncle Matt took in the whole porch with one keen glance.

"You weren't at the tent," he said, "and I wondered where you were."

"I . . . I was busy," Steve stuttered. "Ah . . . working on my project."

"Is this a cage for some sort of animal?" Uncle Matt squatted down beside it.

Steve kept silent, uncertain how to answer. He suspected Uncle Matt knew exactly what it was. He realized he had to be honest. So, haltingly, he told how he and Ron had built the cage and the trap, how don Luís supervised and advised. He was just coming to the part where he had changed his mind about catching a monkey from the forest, how instead he hoped to rescue Eduardo, to save him from the consequences of his mischievous doings.

He didn't get that far in his story. Uncle Matt stood up tall. "I don't like this at all," he lashed out at Steve. "And I don't like your friend Ron. He's encouraging you with these wild ideas."

"No, no! It's all my idea—Ron just helped me. Ron is great—"

"I don't trust him," Uncle Matt interrupted. Turning on his heel, he strode off toward the tent.

Steve's anger flared. "You're wrong!" he yelled. "Ron's my friend! He knows more about monkeys than you'll ever know." He threw down the hammer with a bang. Words he thought he'd forgotten came back to him. "And he's right about a lot of other things, too. Like you making me do all the dirty work! Making a—a servant outta me!" He knew he was talking like a spoiled kid. Right now he didn't care. Uncle Matt wasn't fair. He ought to give a person a chance to explain!

Steve left off work on the cage, but stayed away from the tent till he was sure Uncle Matt had gone back to the building site.

That night, after supper, the two of them had a talk. Rather, Uncle Matt talked and Steve listened sulkily. Once again, his uncle told him why he and his friends bought the rain forest, and how they hoped to protect the animals living in it. "I know you like Ron. I didn't intend to say anything against him. But I've asked about him in town, and nobody knows where he came from or what he really does here. The Smalleys say they've seen him over in their forest, but they didn't notice that he collected leaves. In fact, he didn't have his plant press with him. I just don't know what to make of him."

"I know he's all right," Steve defended Ron stoutly. "Don Luís would know if—I would have noticed if— he's going to send me lots of stuff about monkeys when he gets back to school."

Uncle Matt sighed. "Be careful, is all I'm asking you."

Steve knew he should apologize for the rash things he'd said, but loyalty to Ron prevented him.

"I came home early at lunch to see if you wanted to go with me to the nursery to buy trees and plants for the new yard. The work crew took off to get their rice planted. Until they're finished, I'm doing land-scaping." Uncle Matt stood up. "If the rains hold off—*si Dios quiere*—they'll be back at work before too long. Good night."

Steve sat a while longer before blowing out the lantern. Uncle Matt surprised him using don Luís's favorite expression. He'd heard it often, but never from Uncle Matt. As he thought about it, he actually hadn't talked much to his uncle lately. He hadn't spent much time around the tent either. He'd been too occupied with his friends. But that couldn't be helped, he thought, clenching his jaw with determi-nation. Rescuing Eduardo was the important thing now.

CHAPTER FOURTEEN

BLANCA HATCHED seven baby chicks—
furry balls with yellow legs—three
white, three red, and one gray. Immediately they
followed their mother about the yard, cheeping,
stretching their wings, running. Steve wanted to
hold them and pet them but the small creatures
were raring to go and to grow. They wouldn't be
still. Rojo scratched up worms, and with a shrill,
singsong call, signaled Blanca and the chicks to
come running. The whole yard bustled with activity.

At night, Blanca hopped up on the ladder, calling
the chicks to follow her into the coop. But the babies
couldn't do it—their legs were too short. Steve
caught them one at a time, placing them at the bottom of the log and letting them walk up to the door.
That way he figured they could learn how they were
supposed to go to bed. Rojo went in last, then Steve
secured the door and removed the steps. He had seen
no signs of *el manigordo*, but he resolved not to give
the prowling cat a chance for a chicken dinner.

Sometimes he wished he had gone with don Luís
to the farm. He could have helped with the planting,

and there he wouldn't be troubled with the thoughts that came to mind here in familiar surroundings. He found himself wondering about things he'd been too busy to notice before. Why wouldn't Ron come to the tent to visit Uncle Matt? Whenever Steve had invited him, he laughed and said, "Maybe *mañana.*"

And why hadn't don Luís mentioned to Ron the fascinating collection of stone spheres? He'd told him about most everything else. Maybe don Luís felt the giant stones were too sacred to talk about, even with their good friend. But could this be the reason? Why don't I tell Ron about the stones? he asked himself. That way their friendship would be mended, and things would be the way they used to be—the three of them true friends. But wouldn't that be cheating don Luís?

Steve argued with himself about all this while he rambled alone, exploring and picking *caimitos,* a purple fruit that monkeys liked very much, don Luís had said. Steve liked to eat them too. He was glad that Uncle Matt trusted him to find his way, otherwise he wouldn't have the delicious *caimitos* that grew only in the deep forest. "You've had a good teacher," Uncle Matt said. "Don Luís is the best."

He missed his friends so much, especially don Luís, that he was glad Uncle Matt didn't insist that he stay at the tent all the time. How boring! Without don Luís, however, Steve was careful always to notice where he was and in which direction he was going, so he could find his way back. How terrible to be lost alone in the gloom of the rain forest. He had never thought that way before don Luís left.

But one day, the unthinkable happened. He did not know where he was—every direction looked the same. He could not see the sky through the thick leaves to guess the sun's position. A chill, like a great cold hand, closed tightly around him. Panic seized him just as fiercely as the crying fit had that day at the pool. He wanted to throw down the string bag of fruit and run off every which way.

"Wait a minute," he ordered in a whisper. Forcing himself to stand still, he breathed deeply and deliberately, waiting for calm. When his panic quieted, he began walking in slow motion, looking about for some landmark in the deep, twilit forest.

Ahead of him, he heard a low chuckle, as if some forest spirit found his predicament amusing. From behind him came an answering chuckle. Then in front a louder laugh, answered by an even louder laugh behind him. He stopped, terrified. Who was watching him? Where were they? The laughter continued, increasing in loudness and swirling round him like a maelstrom.

Then Steve remembered. Don Luís and Ron had talked about laughing falcons. Sometimes the birds competed in laughing matches like this one, trying to outdo one another. As Steve stood still, watching first ahead of him and then behind him, he realized he was like a laughing falcon, because the harder they laughed, the faster they whipped their heads around this way and that. From the racket they were making, Steve felt surrounded by thousands of them.

All at once a large bird swooped out of nowhere, down to the ground where a fer-de-lance, blending

with the shadows, lay still. Without a wasted motion, the bird held the snake down with its claw, snapped off its head, then flew to a nearby limb, where it tore off chunks of the long writhing body and swallowed them.

Why, the falcons weren't laughing because he was lost! They were carrying on their falcon business, which had nothing to do with him. What if he had stepped on that fer-de-lance? That would have been the end of everything! He had to wait till his knees stopped trembling. Then he started walking again, keeping a sharper lookout where he put down his feet.

Time passed. As desperately as he tried, he could locate nothing that he remembered seeing before. I wish I could put myself on automatic pilot, he thought. Just let go of the struggle to find my way. He tried it, no hurry, no panic, just a relaxed blankness. On he walked, pretending he knew exactly where he was and knowing he would arrive at the tent in due course, *si Dios quiere*. He smiled, remembering his friend, and slowly the tight core of anxiety in his chest uncoiled and smoothed out like a quiet pond.

CHAPTER FIFTEEN

AHEAD STEVE noticed a light, like sunshine. He didn't know what it could be, but he continued toward it with his same unhurried walk, the same smooth, quiet mind. To his amazement, he soon found himself on the edge of a clearing. That explained the light he'd followed. But it wasn't just any clearing—it was the clearing where the giant stone spheres brooded silently. He caught his breath, more awestruck than the first time he saw the spheres with don Luís. His aloneness caused him to feel a more intense wonder at their majesty and mystery. Standing as still and silent as the spheres, Steve wished for the hundredth time that he could discover their secrets.

In the quiet, he could hear the murmuring river. A joyful relief flooded over him. Now he knew the way back to the tent! All he had to do was go along the river till he found the swimming pool, then follow the path he and Uncle Matt had made from the pool to the tent. Simple. He wanted to sing and shout, but the heavy stillness in the clearing kept him silent.

Before turning toward the river, he took a last look at the Enigmas. A light flashed in his eyes, like a mirror catching the sun rays. Startled, he wondered if the ancient stones were sending him a message, telling a secret to him alone. He held his breath, staring. At the far side of the clearing, where the flash had caught his eye, something moved—a man, in faded jeans and a hat. With both hands he held a shining machete, delicately probing at the base of the largest stone sphere. Ron!

No, no! Steve refused to believe what he saw. Ron was off somewhere, far off. Who could this be that looked like Ron? A mirage! If he stared hard enough, the vision would disappear. He strained his eyes watching, but what he saw didn't vanish. The man searched the ground, every inch, the machete blade catching the sunlight. Every so often, he selected something out of the loosened dirt and examined it. Quickly, he made a decision, either tossing the object aside or putting it in his knapsack. Occasionally he picked up another tool to dig deeper. It appeared to be the small shovel Steve had seen Ron holding that day in town. No doubt about it—this was Ron. And what he was doing wasn't anything a leaf collector would do!

Steve made himself watch long enough to know he was not mistaken. Then soundlessly he turned and made his way toward home. When he reached a safe distance from the sacred ground, where he knew Ron could not hear him, he gave himself over to the racking sobs that had been straining to burst out of him ever since he recognized his friend. He muffled the sounds against the trunk of a cow tree. He felt again the way he had that day at the pool when the monkey screamed with such anguish in fear of him. Ron! Ron! Don Luís must have suspected him from the first. And Uncle Matt held back, not befriending him. How did they recognize Ron, the botanist, for a *huaquero?*

CHAPTER SIXTEEN

IN THE DAYS that followed, Steve didn't know what to do. He worked at his chores like a robot, often suspending motion while he stared at nothing and chewed his lip. He gathered only fruit that grew near the tent, and he dreaded going to the spring. What if he met Ron? What could he say? Should he confront Ron with what he knew? Should he tell Uncle Matt? What should he do?

"Don't you feel well?" Uncle Matt asked one day.

"No. Yes. I'm all right," Steve said hastily.

Another time his uncle guessed, "You're homesick."

"No! No! I'm okay." He knew that his protests sounded too loud to be convincing.

Uncle Matt said no more, but Steve often felt his worried stare. He tried to fill every minute with some activity. Ghost didn't need bathing as often, now that rain fell each night, keeping the dust controlled. Steve found other things to do. Once he carried the black iron pots and the skillet to the spring and scrubbed them with sand until they shone, only to find out from Uncle Matt that he'd ruined them.

"Iron pots are supposed to be black and crusty," his uncle explained, ruefully rubbing his fingers over the smooth, shiny bottoms. "That's what makes them such good pots to cook in."

Steve didn't know what to say. He hoped he wasn't turning back into the muddling boy he used to be.

"Maybe we can salvage them," Uncle Matt continued. "We'll temper them in a hot fire and try starting over, as if they were new." He thought a moment. "Maybe, if you would talk to me before you do anything like this again—"

Steve promised.

He got the spade and headed for the garden to do some digging. He needed to escape the tent, and his mistakes, and his problems that demanded solutions.

Ron didn't come, and he didn't come. Then one day, there he was at the spring, smiling and as friendly as he had been before the event on don Luís's porch. With him he had a worn, old-fashioned doctor bag, one of those that was small at the top where the handle was, then belled out at the bottom. Holes were punched in the side.

"Hey, kid, you'll never guess what I brought you. Come and see!" He picked up the suitcase, and Steve, puzzled but curious, followed him toward don Luís's house. On the way, Steve told about Blanca's chicks, and Ron admired them from a distance as he set down the battered case on the porch. Snapping it open with a flourish, he commanded, "Look inside!"

Steve felt his eyes popping out of his head—a

monkey body lay curled in the suitcase, straggle-haired and skinny. Eduardo!

"Ohhh! Is he dead? No, no!" Steve fell to his knees, staring at the body.

"He's tranquilized. Soon he'll be coming out of it. Better get him in the cage."

Relieved that Eduardo was alive, Steve opened the cage door. Ron reached for the monkey.

"Let me," Steve said.

"Sure." Ron stepped aside.

"Why, he doesn't weigh as much as Blanca!" Steve wailed. Eduardo's eyelids flickered. One of his hind legs twitched.

Steve slid him into the cage and fastened the door. Lying there unconscious, the monkey looked more ragged and forlorn than ever before. Steve watched the slow rise and fall of his bony rib cage while Ron set the suitcase aside and sank down on the step.

"How did you get him?" Steve asked. "What happened?"

"What a comedy!" Ron threw back his head, laughing. "Your monkey went berserk. Bit an old lady. She raised a big fuss. Said she felt herself going mad, foaming at the mouth. Got the police in-volved. The lawyer's secretary went to bat for the monkey—said she'd take him. But just as I suspected, she had nowhere to keep him. Now good ole Ron to the rescue—I told her about your cage and how you were waiting for him. She thought your uncle didn't want him. But I persuaded her—I'm a good persuader." He laughed again. "That's how I got hold of him. The police tranquilized him, the law clerk found the carrying case in the town dump, I guess. And here's your monkey."

"Thank you, thank you for bringing Eduardo," was all Steve could say.

"You owe me, buddy, and don't forget it."

Ron's words scared Steve. They sounded almost like a threat. Quickly he asked, "Will Eduardo be all right? What should I do for him?"

"You have to keep him confined. If he acts in an odd way or gets sick and dies, you must report it. The *señorita* says there's never been rabies here, but you are not to handle him until you're sure he's healthy."

Steve attended Eduardo for the rest of the day, watching him slowly come back to life. He filled a bowl with spring water and picked fresh fruit for him. He had much to think about—how kind señorita Moreno was; she'd kept her word. How kind Ron was to bring Eduardo to him. He would not think about what Ron had said: "You owe me, buddy, and don't forget it." That brought to mind things Steve didn't want to remember. Now he was in Ron's debt as surely as if he'd borrowed a million dollars from him. But I don't care, Steve thought. They would have killed Eduardo. And he's worth more than a million dollars—more than any amount of money. I'll do whatever Ron wants.

Of course, Ron no longer needed to know the location of the stone spheres. He'd found them. Was he buying Steve's silence with Eduardo? No, because

Ron didn't yet know that Steve had seen him at the Enigmas. Steve felt such gratitude that he would not think of the price he might have to pay for the monkey. He wouldn't think of the future at all. He kept busy with Eduardo, giving him the best of care, but he kept wishing that don Luís would return. He'd know of plant medicines that would help Eduardo back to good health.

Steve's wish came true. Don Luís rolled in one morning in an ox cart loaded with many things including bags of beans and rice. His nephew, Tomás, came with him. Ron was nowhere about, but Steve helped them unload. Then don Luís looked at Eduardo, slumped in the corner of the cage. "I will fix him," he said. "He will become a new monkey."

"And a happy one," said Steve.

"That I do not know," don Luís shook his head. "We will wait and see."

Don Luís and Tomás admired the extra touches Steve had added to Eduardo's cage. Don Luís suggested that he carve fruits and flowers on it too, like the ones on his nephew's ox cart. Tomás lent Steve his small pocket knife, and even though he didn't speak English, he taught Steve how to carve with it.

Steve didn't want just any kind of flowers and fruits on the cage; he wanted to carve the ones from the forest around them. That made his work harder, but he kept trying. Don Luís mixed colors for him from the forest plants. To make bright red flowers, Steve borrowed the annatto jar from the tent. All the while he worked, he talked and crooned to Eduardo.

The monkey showed no sign of rabies. However, his gaze seemed always fixed on some far invisible point, and his wrinkled face drooped in sadness. He paid no attention to Steve, or to don Luís as he prepared the tonics from the forest.

"His spirit has left him," don Luís diagnosed. He wouldn't say what Steve knew to be true—Eduardo didn't like being shut in the cage, and he felt afraid in this strange place.

"He's never had such a good life," Ron commented when he returned. Steve noticed that Ron's heavy knapsack made him grunt as he swung it from his shoulders to the ground. He seemed very pleased with himself.

Ron noticed Steve looking. "Rocks," he explained, patting the knapsack. "I found some interesting ones to take to a geologist friend of mine."

Here was a chance for Steve to speak up and tell Ron he knew the "rocks" were really ancient artifacts that belonged to the people of Costa Rica. But he didn't dare. I'll wait till don Luís isn't around to hear, he thought. I don't want to cause trouble for Ron. I just want him to stop digging.

Blanca's chicks grew so fast that feathers were beginning to replace the soft fluff covering them. Don Luís said they were the finest of chickens. When he sat on his porch, they flocked around his feet, making chicken-talk sounds and pecking the floor to let him know they wanted a treat. They liked to sit in his lap, which made Steve laugh. When don Luís napped in his hammock in the afternoons, there was room for the whole family of chickens to take their *siesta* with him, gently swaying in the shade. Many times he complimented Steve on the good job he had done protecting them from *el manigordo*. He gave Steve a sack of beans to take to the tent. "Not pay," he said smiling. "A little gift to feed the uncle."

CHAPTER SEVENTEEN

STEVE WAS SORRY when don Luís's nephew and the big oxen had to go back to their home. Tomás made Steve understand that he wanted him to keep the pocket knife. When Steve protested—he knew that Tomás could not get another one—Tomás grinned and slapped his machete where it hung at his side.

"He is saying he does not need such a small thing. He has his machete," don Luís told Steve. The gift of the knife made Steve happy. Now he could finish carving and painting the cage. He thanked Tomás and added a new phrase he'd learned, *"Que le vaya bien."* It meant "May life go well for you," and that's what he wished for Tomás and the oxen as he told them good-bye.

The tent had been very quiet lately. Uncle Matt still went to the building site every day, but he didn't say anything about the house being finished. Steve and don Luís no longer detoured their morning walks that way because the cage was finished. He'd been so busy learning from Tomás how to carve the decorations and from don Luís how to make the colors, and taking care of Eduardo, too, that Steve forgot the house had anything to do with him. His main concern was that it kept Uncle Matt occupied and away from don Luís's place.

One night Steve asked, "Didn't you say we'd be moved into the house by now?"

Uncle Matt laughed. "I didn't think you'd noticed. Yes, I thought we would be, but I've been working alone. My crew will come back as soon as they can, before the heavy rains start, I hope."

Steve felt guilty that he hadn't been more interested in what Uncle Matt was trying to do. Part of that guilt had to do with Ron. He ought to tell Uncle Matt that he was right about Ron, that Ron wasn't what he appeared to be, and Steve had the proof. Then he realized that he himself wasn't what he appeared to be either. He was living a double life—one at the tent and one at don Luís's house. How disappointed his uncle would be to know Steve was deceiving him! Steve lay awake at night trying to unravel the complications of his life.

What would he do when the workmen came back and moving day arrived? At the new house he'd be so far from Eduardo, he couldn't take care of him every day. If he could move his monkey with him, that would be wonderful. First he had to confess to Uncle Matt what had been going on at don Luís's house. Then his uncle might be so angry that Eduardo was caged, he wouldn't let Steve keep him. What should he do?

Ron liked to needle him about Eduardo. He stressed "can't" and "won't" in whatever he said.

"You know you *can't* take him home with you, don't you? The customs people *won't* allow you to take him out of the country."

Steve suspected that, but he hated hearing it put into words.

"You *can't* leave him here. Don Luís is too old. He *can't* take care of himself, let alone a sick monkey."

That part about Eduardo being sick was no longer true. Steve felt a rush of gladness when he saw how different Eduardo looked now—his body was plump, his hair was clean and shiny. His eyes were still vacant, but as don Luís said, that had more to do with his spirit than his physical health. He and don Luís agreed that it was best to continue feeding Eduardo the healing drinks from the plants and the wild fruits from the forest and to treat him with constant loving care. Steve thought of don Luís as Eduardo's doctor and himself as Eduardo's nurse, in partnership to make him a finer monkey than he'd ever been. He wished the *señorita* could see him. She would be pleased with the change and with the beautiful cage that Eduardo now lived in. Steve wished for a camera to make a photograph for her. He faintly remembered that when he came to Costa Rica, he didn't want a camera.

Ron's reminder that he would have to go back home troubled him. Uncle Matt had already mentioned that his folks wrote in their letters that Steve needed to return in time for the new school year. He'd been here since early in the dry season when he and Uncle Matt slept in the hammocks outside and Ghost had to have weekly baths. Then don Luís left late for the farm because Blanca had disappeared, but fortunately the rainy season had been slow in starting and the planting was accomplished. The building crew had stopped working to plant their rice, too. Finally the rains began, gradually increasing, and the hammocks had to be moved inside the crowded tent. Plants and trees grew like magic— Steve thought he could see it happening. He wouldn't be here for the torrential rains due in October and November, but Uncle Matt had told him about them. After that, the dry season would begin again. Steve knew the pattern of the year so well that Costa Rica seemed more like home than anywhere else. Of course he wanted to see his parents and the rest of his family, but he thought in terms of them coming to Costa Rica rather than him going home.

"Sometime soon," Uncle Matt told him one night, "we'll go to San José. There's business to take care of regarding the forest—preserving it. I have to meet with my partners. While we're there we'll need to set a date for your leaving and confirm plane reservations."

Steve could only stare at his uncle, many thoughts crowding his head. What would happen to Eduardo when he had to leave? Ron was right when he said that don Luís couldn't take responsibility for him. If only he could talk to Uncle Matt about his monkey. But if he told, he'd also implicate Ron and the *señorita*. And what about Ron being a *huaquero?*

Ron continued to plunder the ruins. The stack of "rocks" for his "geologist friend" stretched the knapsack taut, then mysteriously vanished and a new stack started accumulating. Where could he be storing them, or did he have a way of sending them out of the country? Nagged by all his concerns, Steve felt more caged than Eduardo. At least he longed for freedom, while Eduardo seemed not to care one way or the other.

Don Luís had little to say to Ron. Often Steve noticed the older man, his wrinkled face concentrated in a worried frown, watching the younger man. Steve felt that don Luís would like to rid his porch of Ron and all his equipment but didn't know how to do it. He could tell that Ron knew it too, and that he was careful not to overstep certain bounds in the way he acted and what he said, especially to Steve. Almost always when Ron wanted to tease Steve or pressure him about Eduardo, he waited until don Luís was out of earshot.

That was the situation the day Ron asked Steve about San José. Steve was alone on the porch, sitting beside Eduardo's cage, talking to him, when Ron appeared.

"Old pal of mine, is there any chance you and that uncle of yours might be going to the big city soon?"

Steve felt dumbstruck—how had Ron guessed? Did he eavesdrop outside their tent at night?

Ron laughed. "I see 'yes' on your face. That's convenient for me, I can assure you." He sat on the edge of the porch, leaning against a post, before continuing. "Your monkey's doing great—nothing like that weaselly bag of bones I brought to you." He paused.

Steve held his breath, wondering what was coming. "Remember, I told you that rescued monkeys don't come free of charge. I've got a package—a very, very valuable package—that must get to San José soon. I'm counting on you taking it there for me." Ron watched him intently.

Steve looked down, trying to control the trembling inside him. "Why don't you take your package? I might lose it."

"You won't lose it, knowing the consequences." Ron pulled at his lip thoughtfully. "I've gotten word that certain people are watching for me. But they won't suspect a kid. Not even your self-righteous uncle will suspect you." He laughed as if he'd just heard a good joke.

"I . . . I don't know," Steve finally struggled out. "What if I can't? What if Uncle Matt finds out?"

"You can keep that from happening. There's lots of things about you Uncle Matt doesn't know." Ron laughed again. Steve, ashamed that the accusation was true, kept quiet. "You realize, don't you, that the monkey isn't yours till you pay for him? I didn't go to all the trouble of rescuing him for nothing—I knew the day would come when I'd need you bad. Real bad. It's now, kid."

"I don't know about going there—how or when or anything," Steve denied, thinking that at least that much was true.

"Don't forget," Ron's voice was steel hard. "Keep me posted."

CHAPTER EIGHTEEN

MANY TIMES in the days that followed Steve longed to tell his uncle everything. When Uncle Matt glanced up and caught Steve staring at him, he usually said encouragingly, "Is something the matter?"

His uncle seemed so kind then, that Steve almost believed he would understand and help him if he blurted out the whole complicated story. But he remembered how Uncle Matt was against him having anything to do with Ron, and how he was against Eduardo—against everything, it seemed to Steve, as he thought back. And what would happen to Eduardo if he told on Ron? Steve thought of Ron's steely voice and hard laugh and shuddered.

Instead of spilling out the story, Steve said, "How will we get to San José?"

"We have to go into town the afternoon before and stay overnight because our flight to San José leaves at daybreak."

Steve wet his lips. "How long are we staying?"

"A couple of days, unless the paperwork on the land bogs down."

"Okay," Steve said automatically.

"We'll confirm your return ticket and make sure there's space available for you to fly home in about a month. All right?"

"Okay," Steve repeated. Only a month! How could he get everything done, everything solved, in only thirty days? How could he give up Eduardo in four brief weeks?

"I'm hoping you'll be here for the move into the house. I know you haven't been much interested in it, but I think you'll like it. Maybe enough to come back sometime."

"Oh, I will, I do! I'll always want to come back. I don't even want to leave. . . ." Steve protested in his misery.

In the few days before going to the capital, Steve tried to avoid Ron. It was no use; Ron knew Steve's routine too well.

"You're running a risk, you know," Ron told him late one afternoon at Eduardo's cage. "If you don't pay up, your monkey's in trouble—serious trouble. No doubt about it. I wouldn't keep him for a pet— I'm not fond of monkeys."

Steve knew that without being told.

"What's the latest?" Ron pressured him. "When are you off to the big city?"

Steve looked at Eduardo, so handsome and healthy in the big roomy cage. And, to his amazement, Eduardo looked back at Steve! They had never made eye contact before. Steve forgot Ron. He leaned over toward the monkey and began crooning Spanish words to him as the *señorita* had done.

Slowly, Eduardo moved across the cage to Steve, still looking into his eyes.

Steve couldn't believe that at last here was a breakthrough—Eduardo knew him! Eduardo wanted to be friends. He was healing from all the trauma of his life. The monkey reached out a hand to clasp the wire. Steve reached out an answering hand, hoping only to touch Eduardo.

But Ron caught Steve's hand, crushing it in his grip.

"Yowch!" Steve floundered in agony.

Startled, Eduardo retreated.

Ron shoved his face into Steve's. "See, kid, I'm not a patient man. Your bill's come due. When do you go to San José?"

"Five days," Steve gasped, nursing his hurt hand, blowing his breath on the bruised flesh.

"Good! Now listen. The morning before you go, look in the ferns above the spring for a package. It'll be small but valuable—worth the life of an ugly monkey and a boy, I'd say. Priceless, right?"

Steve took a deep breath and stood up. "You know what you're doing is wrong," he said, jutting out his jaw and facing Ron squarely. "It's against the law."

"What do you know about what I'm doing?" Ron grinned maliciously.

"I saw you at the stone spheres, digging," Steve said, steadily holding Ron's gaze.

Ron's laugh held no mirth. "Yeah, I could tell you knew their location. But you and the old man clammed up on me. Then I figured all I had to do was study the routes you took and then sort of average them out. I found the graves too, and a whole lot more. Treasure."

"You're wrong. Why don't you stop? You'll get in trouble."

"One sure thing—it won't be you who'll get me in trouble. Not if you want *el mono* to stay safe, not to mention yourself. It'd be easy for a kid to disappear in the forest without a trace. You know?"

Steve knew, but he persisted. "Why do you do it? What do you get out of it?"

Ron looked at him as if he'd lost his mind. "Money, kid. This is the find of a lifetime. Collectors'll pay a fortune for it. I'll be rich!" He was silent. Then came that malicious laugh. "I might even buy some of this precious rain forest and chop it all down or set it afire. Wouldn't Unca Matt like that!"

Don Luís came into sight along the path from his garden with a load of *yuca* root. Ron turned away, going over to sit on the hollow log and sharpen his machete.

Don Luís set down his produce and called the chickens, ready to put them to bed. Steve started for the tent, knowing he was late. He stepped off the porch, watching Blanca's seven half-grown offspring following her—no, only six trailed their mother. The perky gray one with the red comb and bright yellow legs lingered at the edge of the yard near the bushes, trying to catch one last bug.

What happened next Steve was never able to reconstruct. He was aware only of a rush from the bushes, the flash of a spotted, graceful body, a powerful, large paw upraised, a desperate squawk. Rojo shrilled an alarm, Blanca and the other chickens screamed. In a breath, the predator vanished with the gray chicken. *El manigordo,* without waiting for night, had struck!

Steve sprinted across the yard, too late. Don Luís joined him, but not even a feather remained. They

looked for tracks and found them, large and round. They saw where the animal had waited in the brush, where he'd pounced. They trailed him until his paw prints disappeared in the forest.

Before dark, in front of three witnesses, old Fat Foot had claimed his plump chicken supper! That was unheard of, according to don Luís.

Never again would Steve joke about *el manigordo*— the lethal cat was not funny. Even Ron was shaken. He dropped his flip manner and confessed he'd never seen anything as silent and as swift as the spotted cat. How long had the predator been watching and waiting?

Don Luís began planning a strategy for *el manigordo*'s return. "He will be back for another supper. But next time, make noise. *El manigordo* does not like noise. Yell, beat water buckets, or bellow like oxen. *El manigordo* is not frightened of rocks or sticks, but roaring noises will drive him away."

CHAPTER NINETEEN

STEVE DECIDED to put another layer of wire around Eduardo's cage to make it doubly secure. There was no way now that *el manigordo* could thrust his fat foot through the wire and pull Eduardo out of the cage.

The monkey watched Steve working with a glimmer of interest in his eyes. "You're getting well," Steve rejoiced. "Your spirit's coming back, and you'll soon be a happy monkey, the way I want you to be." All the while he stretched wire and strengthened the door latches and prepared Eduardo for his absence, he talked to him.

Steve didn't know how to warn don Luís against Ron. He believed the less the elderly man knew about Ron's activities, the safer he'd be. Finally, he cautioned his friend to keep himself, the chickens, and Eduardo safe from *el manigordo* and the other dangers of the forest.

I'll be back in maybe three days, he assured himself. What could happen in just three days?

The day they were to leave, Steve found Ron waiting at the spring. "I didn't trust you, kid. You could have said you didn't see the package. Now, you can't deny you got it."

Wrapped in brown paper, it was heavy and well padded. Automatically Steve slipped it under his tee shirt, then stuffed the shirt inside his shorts.

"As soon as you arrive at the San José airport, go to the men's room. Act sick, or make any excuse to escape your uncle for two minutes. My friend will be expecting you. Don't forget—he'll be there."

"How will I know who he is?" Steve asked in a low voice.

"Easy. Check out his hands. Both middle fingers are missing." Ron laughed. "You might ask him why they're missing. It's an interesting story."

From the twist of Ron's mouth, Steve knew it was a story he didn't want to hear.

"How will he know I'm coming?" he almost whispered.

Ron seemed to find his ignorance amusing. "Ever hear of radio? You know, you talk into it, then you say 'over,' and somebody talks back?"

Radio? Where would Ron have a radio? Somewhere at the end of one of his long treks into the forest? "I thought when you talked over radio, everybody could hear what you said," Steve puzzled.

"How about codes? Real cloak-and-dagger stuff." Ron looked pleased with himself. "And the same way—by radio—I'll hear if you deliver or not." He paused. "I may not be here to greet you when you return. But rest assured, I'll be coming." With that warning, Ron left him.

Steve slowly filled the water bucket and returned

to the tent, the parcel weighing like a brick inside his shirt. The dark, sinister face of the man he was to meet haunted him. He pictured a pockmarked face, maybe scarred from countless fights, a sneering mouth, fierce pirate eyes.

Fear of what he had to do made him so miserable he couldn't keep still nor concentrate on anything. He couldn't think what to bring to San José with him besides the sealed packet. Rummaging through the suitcase he'd brought to Costa Rica but never completely unpacked, he found his old windbreaker. That would help conceal the contraband he was carrying to a rendezvous in the restroom at the San José airport.

They planned to leave the tent about mid-afternoon, arriving in town before dark. So many last minute things had to be done, there was no time for Steve to worry. Only when he and Uncle Matt were in the truck, well along the road toward town, did the danger of his position begin moving into focus.

It started when his uncle said, "Whew! In this heat how can you stand wearing that jacket?"

Defensively, Steve pulled the windbreaker closer about him, making sure it disguised the secret in his pocket. "Oh, I'm fine," he said, trying to sound light-hearted, even while he oozed sweat from every pore. "I—I've got a hole in my shirt—a big one—"

He hated himself for lying, for deceiving his uncle. What would Uncle Matt say if "they" arrested him? "They" would send him to prison, and he'd never see his family again. Maybe his family wouldn't want to see him after what he'd done. Sweat rolled down his forehead into his eyes so that he couldn't see out the window to distract himself from his misery.

Uncle Matt said no more about the jacket. They spent the night at the only hotel in town. Steve lay stiff and unsleeping on his side of the bed, the jacket beneath his pillow. The next day, about the time the howlers would be giving their wake-up calls in the forest, Steve and Uncle Matt parked the truck at the small airfield, leaving the key in the ignition, and stood with a half-dozen others waiting for the plane to arrive. They heard it long before it dropped down out of the pale sky.

As soon as the incoming passengers deplaned, those few gathered on the edge of the runway went aboard and chose seats. They were widely scattered, except for Steve and Uncle Matt, who sat together about midway down the aisle. Waiting in the dark, listening for the throb of the plane engine, Steve could pretend that he would never step off the plane in San José, that he would never have to tell another lie, that he would never have to keep an appointment with a sinister man with two missing fingers. Now the realization hit him—the man was probably already waiting at the other end of Steve's flight, watching for him. Now there was no escape, no turning back. All pretense vanished. The picture that began forming in his mind on the trip to town now was in focus, sharp and clear.

His stomach lurched. Too late, too late! pounded inside his aching head. The vibrations of the plane made him sick. Was he going to pass out? He wiped the sweat off his face with his sleeve and doubled over trying to fight off the nausea rising in his throat.

"Airsick?" Uncle Matt leaned near, mouthing the word over the noise of the engines. In agony, Steve shook his head, then nodded. Uncle Matt offered him a piece of gum. "This might help," he said sympathetically.

Steve chewed and chewed, but he grew more and more miserable and afraid.

Uncle Matt watched him anxiously. He held up his wrist, pointing to his watch. "Only forty more minutes. Take off that jacket. You'll feel better."

Steve groaned. He wanted to tell his uncle everything, but he knew that Eduardo's life, and perhaps his own, depended on the safe delivery of the package that was burning a hole in his pocket.

He heard Uncle Matt say, "A hole—," and Steve looked at him in terror, thinking he had read his mind, but then Uncle Matt finished the sentence— "in your shirt doesn't matter. Off with that jacket!" And he seized Steve's collar with one strong hand and began unzipping his jacket with the other.

Steve struggled to his feet, protesting, clutching the jacket to him, but Uncle Matt held on. The plane nosed down, causing Steve to lose his balance and fall. His uncle caught him, but the loosened jacket gave way, releasing his overloaded pocket and dumping the brown parcel in the aisle. It struck the floor with a thump and rolled toward the cockpit. Then, as the plane leveled, the package rolled back, and Uncle Matt's long arm reached for it.

At the same time, Steve, trying to right himself,

grabbed for it too, but his arm was shorter, and his uncle was quicker. He held Steve at bay while he inspected the heavy parcel.

He raised his eyebrows. "What have you got here?"

"Don't open it! Please, Uncle Matt, give it back!"

"What is in this package? The truth, Steve! Now!" Uncle Matt's voice grated in Steve's ears.

Steve sank in his seat. "Give it back, or Eduardo will die," he blurted. "I might die too."

"What has Eduardo to do with this?"

"Eduardo is in the cage at don Luís's house. If I don't deliver this package, Ron will kill him."

"You're delivering this package for Ron?"

"Yes. I have to. I owe him for Eduardo." Steve's chin trembled.

Uncle Matt put his arm around him gently. "Tell me the whole story. Begin now, because there's not much time. Tell everything, and tell it true."

Slowly Steve told him about seeing Ron digging at the Enigmas; about the "rocks" Ron collected for a "geologist friend"; about the rescue of Eduardo and how Steve owed Ron for him; about the man with no middle fingers waiting now in San José. It took a surprisingly short time to tell a guilty secret that had been so long concealed. When he finished, Uncle Matt sat silent, turning the package over and over in his hands as if he could x-ray it with his eyes.

CHAPTER TWENTY

"HOW DO YOU FEEL about being a part of this?" Uncle Matt asked, indicating the package.

Steve answered without hesitation, "I am so sorry that I ever got mixed up in it—that I didn't tell you in the beginning. I've wished a million times over that I could go back and undo what I did." He thought a moment. "If I could do it all over, I don't know how I would change it, though—I had to save Eduardo."

"Yes, I know how much you wanted to help the monkey. But if you cooperate with the authorities, you will lose your friend Ron and maybe your monkey too. People like Ron play hardball for big stakes. You've considered all that?"

"Yes," Steve whispered. "Even if I deliver the package, I know Ron will never be my friend." His voice quavered. "But Eduardo—he's done nothing wrong. It's not his fault. . . ."

"I want to make sure you're going into this with your eyes wide open," Uncle Matt said. "Tell me what you want to do."

"I want to turn in the package to the police. I want to tell them about Ron."

Uncle Matt immediately got up and went to the cockpit, taking the package with him. He was gone about fifteen minutes, shut in with the pilot. He came back still carrying the package and sat down without speaking. Steve looked at him, waiting.

"We've worked out a plan by radio," he said finally. He cleared his throat, as if he didn't like to say what came next. "You are to go ahead—do exactly as Ron told you. Delay giving the man the package as long as you can, to give us time, but don't endanger yourself unnecessarily. He must have the package in his possession when he leaves that room. I won't be far away, and the officials promised to be there, but you know things don't always go according to plan."

The plane began ever so slightly to descend. Uncle Matt glanced out the window. "Plundering ruins and smuggling is a problem in many countries. That's why Ron's case has such far-reaching consequences. That's why turning him in is more important than one friend or one monkey, though I know you can't believe that now. What you're going to do will cost you a great deal, and it'll take courage. You know that?"

Steve nodded.

Uncle Matt squeezed his arm, and then the plane touched down and bumped along the runway. The passengers collected their belongings and moved toward the plane door. Steve put his jacket back on and followed his uncle, who carried their one suitcase. They stepped from the plane into bright sunshine and headed toward the terminal. People seemed to be everywhere, busy doing something, but Steve kept his eyes down. His pocket hung heavy and his jacket, which was much too big for him now that he was leaner, bloused loosely.

Inside, as Uncle Matt paused, Steve forced himself to look around slowly, deliberately, at each of the many faces within his view. Not one of them looked back at him, not one was watching, not one stood out with a dark, heavy-browed face, missing fingers, and criminal intentions.

Uncle Matt led the way to the information desk. Steve knew it was time to make his move. He bent over slightly, holding his stomach with one hand and tugging his uncle's arm with the other. "Stomach-ache," he said grimacing. "Bathroom."

Uncle Matt asked at the desk for the men's room and pointed Steve toward a corridor. "On the left, second door," he called after him. *"Caballeros."*

Steve went with faltering steps to find it. He felt truly sick. With sweating hands he pushed open the door. Instantly he knew he was not alone. He heard a shuffling, then the swishing of water. His eyes adjusted, and he saw a man bent over one of the sinks with his back turned. Black-haired, in a dark suit. Steve stood staring. As the man reached for a paper towel with a five-fingered hand, Steve almost fainted with relief. The man discarded the towel in the waste can, looking at Steve inquiringly.

Steve moved like a sleepwalker to a sink and turned on the faucet. The man glanced in the mirror, smoothed his hair, and left. Steve's big-eyed, yellow-green face looked back at him. He made a quick decision. Slipping the package out of his pocket, he leaned over to conceal it on the floor behind the waste can. Somehow he felt safer not carrying it.

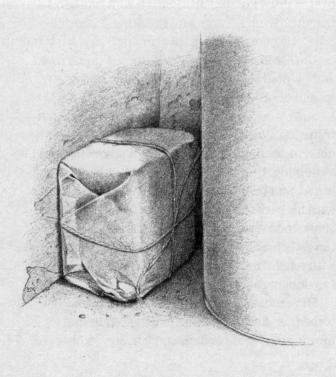

CHAPTER TWENTY-ONE

THE WATER running in the sink looked so cool, Steve turned it on full power and bent to slosh it over his face. How refreshing, like the river pool in the forest. He wished he could be there now! He splattered the water on his eyes, across his face, not caring that it dripped down his neck. He'd forgotten where he was as he turned off the water and reached for a towel. An overpowering scent of ylang-ylang blossoms filled his nostrils.

Steve turned to stone. He hadn't heard the door open. He hadn't heard anyone come in. But a hand closed over his right wrist, a voice said, "The package, please." Steve shook his head, slinging droplets, and blinked furiously to clear his eyes. Even without seeing, he knew that it was only three fingers and a thumb that so powerfully tightened around his wrist. Fingernails dug into his flesh like thorns.

"A towel," he muttered, still reaching, still pretending blindness, forcing the man's hand to move with him to snatch a towel. He dried his eyes and looked directly at the man as he continued wiping his face.

A shock went through Steve. A grandpa! Not his own, but like him—white hair, blue eyes, rosy cheeks. His shirt matched his blue eyes, which were centered with large black pupils. Except for the painful, hurry-up grip on Steve's wrist, he seemed to have all the time in the world.

The ylang-ylang fragrance seared Steve's throat, making him cough.

"Now, my dear boy." The strong grasp of the three fingers and thumb began turning, turning. Fumbling with his free hand, Steve tried to unzip his jacket. "Stall for time," Uncle Matt had said. "We'll be coming." Where were they? Pains shot up Steve's arm. He bit his lip to keep from screaming.

The door opened. A boy Steve's age came in, glancing at them without curiosity. The man relaxed his grip but didn't let go. "You know, dear boy, I'm glad to see you. How are you? How are your parents?" The cordial voice, the hearty chuckle, were the greeting of an old family friend.

When the boy left, the man ran his hands over Steve like a policeman frisking a prisoner.

"Don't tell me you didn't bring it," he said softly, dangerously, going back over Steve, searching.

"Yes, yes, I have it," Steve breathed. "But how do I know you're the right one?"

"You know. You were told." The man glanced around, searching the room with his eyes. He seized Steve's hand, crushing it as Ron had that day at don Luís's, then turned Steve's arm so that it popped in its socket—turning, turning. Yet his face remained like a kindly grandpa's.

Steve clenched his teeth against the pain. Surely Uncle Matt and the officials would be here any minute. He listened, praying that the door would open.

"I'll get it." If he delayed any longer, he knew his arm would break.

"Your last chance," the man said. He released his hold. Steve's relief was so great his knees almost gave way. He rubbed his arm, leaned down, and retrieved the parcel from behind the waste can.

The man took it triumphantly, fingering the shape of it, hoisting its weight.

"Are you sure it's the right package?" Steve asked.

"You wouldn't dare change it." He tore his hungry gaze away from the brown parcel, looking at Steve with a tinge of doubt in his face.

"Ron might've sent the wrong one," Steve suggested.

"Such things have happened," the man agreed. "Let's see what you brought me." A smile curled the corners of his mouth. "It'll take only a moment." Deftly he slipped a long sharp fingernail the length of the package like a letter opener and rolled back the paper. Soft kapok spilled out. As he brushed it aside, Steve saw gold gleaming in the nest of fluff.

There lay the most beautiful man-made object Steve had ever seen—a plump gold monkey standing on two feet with his tail curling round his shoulders. He looked out of the kapok with the confident and happy expression Steve had seen so often on Clown's face.

Steve gasped. He couldn't help it. He was struck

by such a sudden, painful yearning to possess that gold monkey, to have it be his alone. The man also stared at the monkey, and Steve saw his own raw greed reflected in the man's face. He shut his eyes against it.

"Genuine pre-Columbian," the man murmured with satisfaction.

When Steve opened his eyes, the packet had disappeared. The man dusted a fluff of kapok from his suit and turned to go.

"Thanks, dear boy," he said over his shoulder.

The door opened and then shut, but not before Steve heard a voice of authority speaking in formal Spanish, addressing the *señor*. He knew he was hearing the voice of the law, the voice that doomed Eduardo, and perhaps himself. He sank to the bathroom floor. That's where Uncle Matt, rushing in with a policeman, found him.

With great care, Uncle Matt lifted him to his feet and held him close for a moment. "Well done, Steve," he whispered.

CHAPTER TWENTY-TWO

THEY SPENT six worry-filled days in San José, far longer than Steve had expected. All the while that he was questioned by the authorities, telling everything he knew over and over, he wondered what was happening back in the forest. While accompanying Uncle Matt from government office to government office, working through forms and papers to set up a trust for the protection of the forest, Steve wondered if Eduardo was safe. In the evenings when they visited the homes of Uncle Matt's partners to discuss the study center and plan its future, Steve hardly realized where he was.

He knew the authorities were doing everything possible to catch Ron. By radio, they notified the police in Los Cocos and warned them of danger to don Luís and Eduardo. Every day Uncle Matt and Steve checked with the officials for news. Not until the fifth day did word come that the policemen assigned to pursue Ron had learned he'd left town about a week ago for the Smalleys' forest. They immediately set out to search for him.

Steve felt dazed with relief when he realized what this meant. From the time he and Uncle Matt left for San José, Ron headed away from don Luís's in an entirely different direction. Don Luís and Eduardo were safe!

Their last day in the capital, they confirmed reservations for Steve's return to the United States on September 1. On that date he would have to say good-bye to the forest, to Uncle Matt, to don Luís, and to the monkeys.

They boarded the small plane that took them south across the mountains, jungles, and forests to the airfield where they had left the old red truck. Steve was barely aware of the return trip. He could think of nothing except seeing don Luís and Eduardo again. Once, in an unguarded moment, Ron's words at the spring that last morning ran through his head: "I may not be here to greet you when you return. But, rest assured, I'll be coming." The threat implied in his words had lost its power. He'd never have to be afraid of Ron again. He couldn't wait to get back!

During the drive from Los Cocos to the tent, Uncle Matt reassured him once more of the safety of his friend and his pet. Then he added, "I'll help you find a home for Eduardo. The Smalleys might take him."

"Mrs. Smalley doesn't like Eduardo," Steve objected.

"In the cage, as you have him now, she wouldn't mind him. Ideally, he should be trained to take care of himself so he could return to the wild."

Steve agreed that would be best. He would like to

see Eduardo as happy as Clown and his troop. But even if other spider monkeys could be found, it was doubtful they would accept Eduardo. For the present, though, Steve was content to solve that problem another day.

Late in the afternoon they drove into the tent yard. As soon as they unloaded the truck, Steve grabbed the empty water buckets and headed for the spring and don Luís's.

"Hold on a minute," Uncle Matt ordered. "I think it best that I go with you until we know for sure that Ron is caught."

For a fleeting moment, Ron's promise, "I'll be coming, . . ." shook Steve's confidence. But he remembered the two policemen who had been dispatched to the Smalleys' to catch Ron, and he felt better. He waited impatiently while Uncle Matt got a bucket and joined him on the path to the spring. They passed the ylang-ylang tree, still spangled with pale green blooms perfuming the air with heavy, sweet fragrance that now brought only pain to Steve.

They left their buckets at the spring and hurried to don Luís's house. Even before they reached it, Steve became aware of a strange lack of activity— no busy chickens scratching in the yard, no don Luís digging *yuca* in the garden. A chilling silence gripped the familiar scene. Rojo and Blanca's coop, to one side of the house, stood empty, the door unlatched. He took the steps in one leap to Eduardo's beautiful carved cage on the porch. Empty. He blinked his eyes, dropping to his knees to peer inside the loose-swinging door.

"What does this mean?" he cried.

"Don Luís!" Uncle Matt called.

A great fear clamped hold of Steve. He turned toward Uncle Matt, who said, "Inside! Hurry."

At first, the neatness of don Luís's one room seemed undisturbed. The dried herbs and leaves still hung from the rafters, the seeds and roots were spread on the table.

"Don Luís!" Uncle Matt shouted urgently.

"Don Luís!" Steve echoed.

A faint groan answered them. They searched the room, discovering a dark smear, like old blood, that led them to where the elderly man had dragged himself, as if to hide, under the table.

Curled in a knot, arms and legs bound, mouth taped shut, don Luís lay with his eyes closed. They moved the table from over him, spilling some of the seeds in their hurry, and carried his limp body with careful steps to the porch, where they could see better. Blood matted his gray hair, staining it the color of mud.

Working quickly, Uncle Matt cut the ropes and set Steve to chafing don Luís's wrists and ankles to restore circulation. Gently, bit by bit, Uncle Matt removed the tape from the wrinkled brown face. Don Luís groaned again, but his eyes remained shut.

Steve sprinted to the spring for water to bathe don Luís's face and cleanse his stiff hair. With the dried blood washed away, they found two gashes in his head, which began oozing blood again. Uncle Matt ran to the tent for the first aid kit, containing bandages and antiseptic. When don Luís was neatly doctored and bandaged, they lifted him into his hammock, which they had moved inside for safety.

"It's not as bad as I thought at first," Uncle Matt comforted Steve. "I believe he'll come out of this. But we'll have to stay with him round the clock." He looked out the door into the forest. "Unless he recovers, we'll never know what happened."

Steve vowed to himself he would do everything to make his friend well. He lighted a fire in the little stove and set a pot of water on to heat. He found don Luís's healing tea mixture that had restored life and spirit to Eduardo. He measured a tablespoon into a cup, ready to pour in the warm water and begin dosing him as soon as don Luís became conscious.

Steve and Uncle Matt talked very little. They were both too occupied with their thoughts. Uncle Matt sat in the dark on the porch, watching, while Steve sat beside don Luís in the lamplight.

Steve dozed, then jerked himself awake to find don Luís staring at him. His friend whispered something. Steve leaned closer.

"*El manigordo,*" Steve understood him to say. What did that explain? *El manigordo* couldn't beat old men on the head and open doors to monkey cages and chicken coops. But he knew that don Luís shouldn't talk until he was stronger. He hurried to mix the remedy and, using a spoon, persuaded don Luís to drink a little.

CHAPTER TWENTY-THREE

OFF AND ON for the rest of the night, every time don Luís stirred, Steve coaxed him to swallow a few spoonfuls of liquid. By the time the howlers greeted the day in the forest, don Luís slept quietly, his chest rising and falling evenly.

Uncle Matt found an extra hammock, which he strung up on the porch where Ron's hammock used to hang. "You sleep now," he ordered Steve. "You'll need to rest for your watch tonight."

Steve felt too tired and bewildered to protest. He knew, as he lay down, that he and don Luís were safe with Uncle Matt on guard. Still, he could not fall asleep right away. The yard and the house were too silent and still. His eyes kept coming back to the empty cages.

"*El manigordo,*" don Luís had whispered. It couldn't be old Fat Foot. Here was a mystery he could not solve. How could he wait to hear from his friend what happened? The hammock swayed softly, the warm air soothed him. He fell asleep watching the decorated, but empty, monkey cage, its door swinging expectantly.

During the next few days Steve learned a lot about his uncle, who cared for don Luís as if he were his own dad. Steve didn't know Uncle Matt spoke such fluent Spanish until he heard him talking with the elderly man, now too dazed to express himself in English.

Steve wished with all his heart that he could understand don Luís's story, which he told brokenly and with tears rolling from the corners of his eyes as he lay in his hammock. Steve caught Ron's name, but couldn't recognize the other words. When don Luís finished, they gave him more of the healing potion. Then Steve sat beside him, rocking the hammock like a cradle, till he fell asleep again.

"That's good," Uncle Matt said. "Sleep helps him get well."

On the porch, Uncle Matt said in a low voice, "From what don Luís told me and from what we already know, this appears to be the story. Ron spread the rumor in town that he was headed for Smalleys' forest. Instead, he waited at his radio—wherever that is—until he learned you had caused the collector to be caught and the gold monkey was in the custody of the police. Then he hiked back here. During the night he attacked don Luís, tying him up and opening the cages so the spotted cat could finish off the animals. Apparently he was in too big a hurry to take the time required to drag them out and kill them himself. Don Luís heard *el manigordo* come—the chickens and Eduardo put up a terrible fight. Don

Luís remembers the monkey screaming and the chickens shrieking for help, but he couldn't get loose. He managed to squirm his way under the table, hoping to be hidden if Ron returned. That's the last he remembers."

Steve laid his head on his knees, sitting there on the steps, and imagined that awful night.

"I've sent word to Tomás about his uncle. He must stay with you and don Luís while I go into town to report what's happened. We need to know if Ron has been caught—we can't feel safe as long as he's roaming the forest."

As soon as Tomás and the oxen arrived, Uncle Matt left for town in the red truck. Tomás heard the account of Ron's night attack from don Luís with solemn expression. Afterward, he went to Eduardo's cage and laid his hand sorrowfully on the carved fruits and flowers.

Now that his nephew was here, don Luís seemed to recover faster. He helped Steve mix the health-giving teas that he drank and seemed to regain hope. Though Steve was heavy-hearted and Tomás was afraid, they kept the el-derly man entertained with tales and jokes. Don Luís could walk about on his own again, and they spent most of the day on the porch and in the yard.

A few days after Uncle Matt left, Steve sat on the

old log on the edge of the yard peeling a stalk of sugarcane that Tomás had brought with him. The two men relaxed on the porch steps, sharpening their machetes. For the first time since returning from San José, Steve talked about Eduardo. Now that he was certain don Luís would live, he needed to put into words how much he missed his pet. He knew his friends understood his sorrow even though Tomás did not speak English.

As the words poured out, an aching regret squeezed his chest. His eyes burned with unshed tears, and his voice trembled. "Eduardo, Eduardo!" he said, leaning his face against the cane stalk.

Suddenly, he became aware of the strange silence on the porch. His friends sat still, their hands in midmotion with their sharpening files. They stared at him, their brown faces lax with foolish smiles.

Steve was confused by their happy expressions. He had blurted out his secret feelings, and they thought he was funny! Don Luís and Tomás didn't seem to understand. How stupid he felt to be seen crying over his pet.

Something tugged at his tee shirt. Wiping the tears from his eyes with the back of his hand, he glanced down. Beside him on the log, looking up into his face, sat Eduardo, as thin and unkempt as when he lived in town.

Every tear dried instantly. Steve was seized by such surprise and joy, he thought the top of his head would blow off. He felt like doing everything that he must not do—jump up and shout; laugh hysterically; faint and fall off the log—all at the same time. Yet he

knew that any one of these reactions would scare
Eduardo back into hiding.

Instead, Steve made himself say softly, his voice
singing, "Eduardo, Eduardo, my little spider monkey, Eduardo. Are you hungry? I will get a banana
for Eduardo." He talked to the monkey the way he
used to talk when he sat beside the cage. Slowly, he
stood up and moved to the porch, where he laid
down the stalk of half-peeled sugarcane and took
two bananas out of the bunch hanging from the
rafters. His friends on the steps—the first to know
the great news that Eduardo was alive—watched,
without talking or moving, while Steve returned to
the old log and offered a banana to Eduardo.

Without hesitating, the monkey accepted it,
peeled it with care, and then began to eat. Using the
same tone of voice that he spoke with to Eduardo,
Steve talked to his beaming friends. "I think he
should go back into the cage at night to be safe. Do
you think so, don Luís?"

"Sí, for fear of el manigordo. I do not know how he
escaped that night, unless señor Fat Foot was too
busy eating my Blanca and my Rojo and the young
chickens." In the midst of his happiness over
Eduardo's return, Steve felt a pang of sadness for his
friend's loss. He realized that not all the creatures
could have escaped the spotted cat. What a miracle
that Eduardo had survived and had come back!

Quietly and without hurry, Steve put fresh water
in the carved and decorated cage on the porch and
piled in the bananas. Soon, with coaxing, Eduardo
swung into his bedroom, and Steve shut and latched

the door. The monkey drank and ate as if he'd had very little since he went into hiding. Steve watched over him until dark came, then with the help of his friends moved the cage beside his hammock. Faintly, he could hear don Luís and Tomás still chuckling as he drifted off to sleep.

CHAPTER TWENTY-FOUR

AWAKENED by the howlers at dawn, Steve thought he'd had a wonderful dream until he saw the cage with Eduardo inside still sleeping. It was true—Eduardo had returned! He and don Luís agreed that from now on Eduardo could be free during the day. As he had not run away after the fight with *el manigordo,* they knew he would continue to stay close to don Luís's house. This had become home to him. Steve marveled that Eduardo trusted him enough to come back to him after such a terrible fright. Before long, Eduardo remembered that he could trust don Luís too. Gradually he was willing to accept Tomás, but he remained wary of Uncle Matt when he returned from town.

After Uncle Matt recovered from his surprise over Eduardo, he told them, "The news is not good. Police have found no trace of Ron—he's disappeared completely." His forehead wrinkled with worry. "When I heard that, I floorboarded that old truck back to the forest, afraid he'd return to finish the job he started."

Why had Ron left them in safety? Was he

watching, like *el manigordo,* waiting for his chance to pounce?

"The officials in San José radioed that the collector you helped them catch is a big-time international dealer in pre-Columbian artifacts," Uncle Matt continued. "He used to be a *huaquero* himself down in South America until he double-crossed his coworkers. They punished him by forcing him to chop off his own middle fingers with a machete. They figured, I guess, that he'd be branded for life, wherever he went."

"But he can't go anywhere now," Steve said. "Can he?"

"He's got a string of crimes behind him, including murder—enough to keep him locked up for a long time. But Ron is still free. And he won't forget he lost his big chance because of you. That's what worries me."

Sitting in the warm darkness of don Luís's porch, they talked to relieve their anxiety. Every unexpected sound from the forest caused their voices to falter and Steve's heart to skip a beat. Don Luís asked to hear again, for the hundredth time it seemed to Steve, about when he saw Ron digging at the great stone spheres. And he wanted to hear once more the description of the gold monkey. Steve discovered he could talk about the monkey now without any desire to have it for himself. Uncle Matt had told him that eventually the artifact would be exhibited in a public museum for all the people to see. Steve knew that was where it belonged.

With Eduardo roving about the yard and house

during the day and sleeping safely in his cage each night, Steve felt satisfied. He said to the others in the dark of the porch, "I want to get a special treat for Eduardo. I think tomorrow I'll go find some *caimitos* for him. You remember, don Luís, there's a tree not far from the Enigmas."

Uncle Matt stirred uneasily. "You must not go anywhere alone until . . ." He left unspoken the danger that threatened Steve.

In the silence, don Luís spoke slowly. "I have had many thoughts lately about this situation. I am believing the stone spheres may help us know the mystery of Ron. I will go with you tomorrow to find *caimitos*—early."

After a while, Uncle Matt cleared his throat. "If you think, don Luís, that the stone spheres can provide an insight into this situation, I too will go tomorrow. Tomás, will you stay with Eduardo?" He repeated his request in Spanish to make sure Tomás understood.

And so it was arranged. They wasted no time getting into their hammocks. Steve could hardly sleep, his thoughts tumbled about in his head so fast, round and round, over and over. What an eerie thing for don Luís to say. Cold chills broke out on his arms as he heard again the formal, almost stilted, way the two men had talked, telling each other more than the words alone said. Trying to understand what it might be was like beating his head against one of the Enigmas. Finally, knowing he had to be up early, he made himself think of Eduardo, sleeping in his cage within reach of Steve's hand. Then he slept.

In the semidarkness of the forest dawn, they swung off, Steve and Uncle Matt following don Luís's lead. Steve noticed he was the only one with a string bag hanging from his shoulder, though the others wore their machetes. He knew that don Luís and Uncle Matt, through some silent communication he could not fathom, intended to do something other than picking fruit for the monkey.

He knew, too, that the plan the men had made included him. Today the three of them would take action to clear up this mystery threatening them, the mystery that no one else had been able to solve for them. Into the deep forest they were going, to the Enigmas, with a purpose that allowed no slowing of pace, no resting along the way. Steve felt the strength of his legs as he kept pace with the men. He liked the easy movement of his body, which had no excess weight now to slow him down.

When they reached the *caimitos*, Steve found the tree almost bare of the purple, plum-size fruit and realized the season was past. He ate one and gathered a half-dozen others. Uncle Matt and don Luís unwrapped banana leaves from tortillas and chunks of white cheese, which they'd carried in their pockets for a quick lunch to share with him. Afterward they drank water from Uncle Matt's canteen and continued on their way.

Steve was last to step into the clearing when they reached the Enigmas. As always before, a feeling of awe overwhelmed him. He could hardly raise his eyes to look at them. When he did, he saw that everything seemed the same.

Without thinking, he moved toward the largest sphere where he'd seen Ron digging that day. He heard a groan, but he didn't believe it. Don Luís and Uncle Matt, close behind him, rushed ahead. Steve saw a man's body pinned to the ground by the giant sphere, which covered the man's arm and appeared to be crushing his shoulder.

He knew instantly the familiar faded jeans and the sun-bleached hair, but he couldn't recognize the swollen face and neck, dark with bruises. Ron had kicked and thrashed with such violence that one of his boots had been slung off. His free hand had groveled in the dirt—the nails were split, his fingers bleeding. Around him hung a cloud of sickening stench that made Steve want to gag and turn away. Yet he felt a great sorrow for Ron's suffering, and he wanted to help him.

He could see how Ron's bleared eyes tried to focus on them. "Help! Please help me!" His voice, hoarse from hopeless calling, pleaded. As they knelt beside him, trying to understand what they should do, Ron's expression changed as his confused mind seemed to identify Steve. His mouth twisted in the familiar ugly way, and curses exploded from his lips.

"Save your strength," Uncle Matt commanded. "You're going to need it for other things."

First Uncle Matt gave the fevered man a drink from the canteen. Ron wanted more, but Uncle Matt said he must not drink too much too fast.

"The pain—I can't stand it," Ron said in a long, drawn-out groan. "Thirsty—hungry—"

"How long have you been pinned here?" Uncle

Matt asked, clearing space around Ron, getting ready for whatever they would do. Steve could see no way to get Ron from under the rock.

"I don't know," he whispered. "Not been conscious all the time—not sure."

Uncle Matt gave him more water. Steve ran to the river, dipped his tee shirt in, and raced back with it dripping wet to bathe Ron's bloated face. Don Luís had disappeared.

"Give him another drink," Uncle Matt ordered, walking about, studying the sphere from all sides. Ron groaned at the effort to swallow.

"How did it happen?" Uncle Matt squatted beside Ron.

"The two poles—I used them as levers to pry the stone out. Each time I moved it back, I shoved the third pole under crosswise to hold it off me while I pried some more. When I started digging, something went wrong—musta weakened my support. Just as I reached under for—," he hesitated, squinting his eyes at Steve, "for something, all hell broke loose. It caught me—" A terrifying groan shook him. "Do something! Help me—"

Don Luís came back with a handful of leaves. "Chew these," he ordered, putting them to Ron's cracked lips. Without questioning don Luís's judgment, Ron used his free hand to stuff the leaves in as if they were food. He chewed eagerly, knowing, as Steve did, that don Luís's forest wisdom would give him relief from pain.

CHAPTER TWENTY-FIVE

Now the three of them set about prying the stone sphere off Ron by using the levers he had cut from saplings. Each time they succeeded in lifting the stone a little, they shoved rocks underneath to hold the sphere in that position, until they levered it back farther and shoved more rocks underneath. They took special care not to touch the crushed arm they were exposing.

As they heaved and sweated, Uncle Matt commented, "Remember Archimedes? He claimed if he had a place to stand on, he could use a lever like this to move the earth."

Steve didn't know about anybody named Archimedes, but it seemed to him that moving the earth might be as easy as trying to move this huge stone sphere. But moving it they were, little by little, *poco a poco*. Ron slipped into oblivion, whether from the leaves he'd chewed or the pain he was enduring, they couldn't tell. How much easier it was to do what they had to do without hearing his heart-wrenching groans!

Uncle Matt kept a watchful eye on don Luís. Steve

knew he was concerned that the older man would overexert himself rescuing the one who had battered him so severely. Steve worked all the harder, wanting to spare his elderly friend; he didn't talk, but just listened carefully and did immediately what he was told to do. His questions would have to be asked later. He felt proud that his uncle was so strong, that he knew how to go about this difficult job. He was proud that Uncle Matt knew about Archimedes, and Steve vowed he'd find out about him too.

They reached a point where Uncle Matt said, for safety's sake, they could roll the stone no farther. Now they must dig with Ron's shovel around and under his arm and hand, which was still pinned by the rock, until they could drag him free. Panting and dripping with sweat, they at last pulled Ron clear. Even in his unconscious state, he moaned pitifully. Uncle Matt gave the arm a brief examination, running gentle fingers along the length of it.

"What a lucky fellow," he said. "The soft, dug-up earth allowed his arm to sink under the weight of the stone. It's damaged, but I don't believe he'll lose it."

Steve threw himself down to look under the stone, straining his eyes to see what Ron was reaching for when the accident happened. He could see nothing clearly—no shape, no size—just a faint gleam of gold in the dirt. Perhaps another gold monkey to replace the one he tried to sell to the collector? "Money, kid. I'll be rich," he'd bragged.

They lowered the stone sphere, little by little, back into its ancient bed and scattered the rocks that had served as props. They bound Ron's injured arm on a makeshift brace. Working fast, they cut fresh saplings the same size as Ron's levers. With stout vines they lashed the timber together into a water-tight raft onto which they loaded Ron as the day was waning.

"We have to travel light," Uncle Matt directed. "Hide the canteen and his stuff. They'll rust away if we never come back. We'll eat the *caimitos.*"

Last, Steve stuffed his string bag into the hiding place. Then they slid the raft into the river with Ron stretched full-length down the center. Uncle Matt held the raft against the tug of the current while don Luís and Steve hunched down and crawled carefully aboard, keeping the craft balanced. Uncle Matt, crouching low, came on last with his navigating pole. Seated in front, he held them at midstream as well as he could in the dark and guided them around boulders and past logs as the current swept them downstream toward the swimming pool.

Don Luís and Steve sat like Buddhas, never stir-ring, though Steve, now that he was still, felt limp with exhaustion. Soon, however, he became en-grossed in their journey along the dark river. Noises from the forest pounded his ears, yet he could hear Uncle Matt's pole when it grated against a boulder. Sometimes, if the raft began spinning, or if the cur-rent carried it too fast, Uncle Matt dug the pole into the bottom until their balance was restored.

Steve didn't realize they'd reached the pool until his uncle poled the raft against the shore. Again, Uncle Matt anchored them while don Luís and Steve crawled stiffly onto the rocks. Then all three of them dragged the raft ashore. Uncle Matt checked Ron's breathing by feeling the rise and fall of his chest.

"Good," he said. "Now we'll convert the raft into a stretcher." They removed all the logs except the ones Ron rested on, and they bore him along the path toward the tent—Uncle Matt in front, don Luís and Steve at the rear. How glad Steve was that they had kept the path cleared! Otherwise they might not have reached the truck with their load.

As it was, they found the truck with the key in the ignition as Uncle Matt always left it. With effort, they shoved Ron in the back, tucked a cover around him, and Uncle Matt drove away toward town. Steve and don Luís watched the taillights disappear, then made their way along the familiar path in the darkness, past the fragrant ylang-ylang tree, to the spring where they drank. Back at don Luís's house, Tomás had the lamp burning, and beans and rice were ready for them to eat.

Before going inside, Steve stood beside Eduardo's cage, running his hands over the carved decorations and testing the double latches. He could not see Eduardo because of the night, but he knew he was sleeping. He wished he could tell him the great news that they were all now safe from Ron and the collector with the missing middle fingers. He thought only fleetingly of the gold hidden forever under the big stone sphere. He felt thankful to be here with his real monkey and with his friends, and he fervently hoped Uncle Matt would get Ron to the doctor and soon be back in the forest.

CHAPTER TWENTY-SIX

DURING THE DAY, Eduardo used don Luís's yard as his playground. He leaped from tree to tree, every so often swinging in on the porch to see what was happening and helping himself to a banana. He followed Steve and don Luís to the garden, where he watched what they did and tasted what they harvested. He hopped from the back of one ox to the other while Tomás fed them.

"It's like he's lived here all his life," Steve said happily late one afternoon, watching Eduardo run along a tree limb at the edge of the yard. Tomás sat on the steps mending the oxen harness while don Luís, using the single-stick loom, wove a string bag to replace the one Steve left at the Enigmas. Steve was idle, watching for Uncle Matt to come striding along the path with news of Ron. They had been expecting him all day. *El manigordo* was farthest from their thoughts, but in a breathless instant, his spotted body and long, beautiful tail took shape in the dappled sun and shade at the end of the hollow log.

Before Steve could move or shout a warning to the monkey, Eduardo also saw *el manigordo*. An

amazing thing happened—Eduardo began an un-
earthly screaming and came tearing through the
trees to a low limb directly above *el manigordo*.
Breaking off a leafy branch, he flailed the limb he sat
on, all the while peering down at the spotted cat and
screeching with rage. *El manigordo* flattened his ears,
glaring above him at the threatening monkey. Then
the cat seemed to shrink, and he slunk away, his
long tail trailing.

"Wow!" Steve exclaimed, jumping off the porch
and calling to Eduardo. "You scared me to death,
raising such a ruckus. You scared Fat Foot, too!"

Don Luís said, "That is what I heard the night I
thought Eduardo was killed."

Eduardo climbed down onto the hollow log but
refused to come to Steve. He seemed to have something on his mind.

"That must be how he escaped that night—he
scared *el manigordo* off," Steve decided, watching the
monkey hop to the ground and bend over to look
into the log. "You told me once that *el manigordo*
didn't like loud noises, that I should beat a bucket to
scare him." He said admiringly to Eduardo, "You
sounded worse than a thousand beat buckets!"

What a neat monkey, he thought. Look how curious he is, spying into the log. What's in there? He
went to see. Don Luís and Tomás followed him.
Steve, peering around the monkey's head, could see
only darkness in the log, but Eduardo continued to
look, moving closer so that his head was inside the
hollow.

"I can't see anything," Steve said, puzzled, "but

I hear something like . . ." He stood back so that don Luís could look in with Eduardo. "Remember that day we were sitting on the log, when Blanca was missing?" That was it! Chickens!

Don Luís backed away from the log in astonishment. "This I cannot believe!" Over his shoulder he said rapidly, "Bring rice! Bring corn! A coconut!"

Tomás and Steve ran. Tomás split a coconut with his machete, and Steve brought dried corn and rice from the house. By the time they returned, Eduardo was sitting on top of the log, watching don Luís patting and stroking Rojo and Blanca. The chickens were having trouble standing, they were so weak.

As soon as the grain was scattered at their feet and the coconut halves set down, the hen and rooster began their high-pitched calls that had always signaled, "Food! Come and get it!" to the younger chickens. And there, standing uncertainly in the opening of the log, was one of Blanca's chicks. When it tottered to the ground, another appeared, looking dazed. Eventually all six of Blanca's offspring clustered around the coconut or pecked at the grain. The entire chicken family was together again!

What a happy going-to-bed time for everybody that night, especially for don Luís.

"I can't wait to tell Uncle Matt," Steve said. "He won't believe it."

But Uncle Matt did believe it. "Missing so many days!" he marveled. He closed his eyes tight and tapped his head. "I'm remembering something that happened to your grandpa. A blizzard came unexpectedly when he was growing up on the farm in

Minnesota. A whole flock of chickens disappeared in the storm. Your grandpa looked for them everywhere, for—I think it was two weeks. Ask him when you get home. Anyway, one sunshiny day, here they came flopping out of a snow bank, every one of them safe and sound."

Steve had never heard his grandfather talk about growing up on the farm. Here was another question to add to the long list of things he intended to learn more about. After they had talked themselves out about the chickens and Eduardo, Uncle Matt told them what happened to Ron.

"The doctors say his arm will be all right after a long period of therapy. But his looting days are over. When the law finishes with him, he'll never come back to the forest."

During the evenings on the porch, they told and retold the terrible and wonderful things that had happened. In each telling, one of them recalled some new bit of information so that the story continued to grow. But during the day, don Luís worked at his house and garden, while Tomás and his oxen helped Uncle Matt and Steve move to the new house overlooking the *Golfo Dulce*. Uncle Matt drove the truck piled with heavier items, while Steve and Tomás followed with the food supplies and kitchen utensils in the ox cart.

When they finally unloaded everything and set the house in order, it was time for Tomás to say good-bye. He was leaving for his home the next day, but he would come again soon to see how don Luís was getting along.

Sleeping in a house seemed strange to Steve after living so long in the tent and on don Luís's porch. But he knew that the new house, with its more civilized comforts, was good preparation for his return home.

In the time he had left, he often hiked to don Luís's to visit with him and to play with Eduardo. He spent his last night there, sleeping in his old hammock near Eduardo's cage. In the morning, first thing, Steve opened Eduardo's door while don Luís let the chickens out of their coop. Such crowing and clucking and chattering! The yard took on new life with Eduardo and the chickens starting their day.

When Uncle Matt blew the truck horn at the old tent site, Steve told don Luís good-bye. "I'll come back," he promised.

Don Luís, with a shy smile, produced a gift for him—a bright-colored woven string bag filled with an assortment of Steve's favorite fruits. "To eat along the way," he said.

Steve gave his friend a quick hug. He took a last look at the little house, the two cages, the hollow log, and Eduardo and the chickens, imprinting his mind with every detail. Turning, he ran along the path past the spring. He was sorry not to see Clown and his troop of squirrel monkeys again, but with Uncle Matt there to protect them, he knew he'd see them next time. Past the ylang-ylang tree he ran and then jumped into the truck.

"When you come back," Uncle Matt said, shifting gears, "this spot will be so overgrown you won't be able to find where the tent stood."

In town, Steve helped with errands until afternoon, when he went alone to visit the *señorita*. They talked for a long time. He told her how well everything had turned out for Eduardo and thanked her for saving him. At that point, they fell silent, both of them thinking, Steve knew, of Ron, but they did not mention his name. Before saying good-bye, Steve told her about his plans to study Spanish and become an expert on monkeys. "Then I want to come back to Costa Rica someday."

"That is wonderful," she said. "You must come to see me when you return." From her desk drawer she took a small box. "So you won't forget," she said, handing it to him.

Steve didn't know proper etiquette—whether he should open the package now or later. However, he didn't hesitate long. Off came the lid, revealing a hand-carved wooden monkey. Not a gold one, but a natural-looking rain forest monkey, the kind he liked best. Its brown fur looked real, and its bright eyes, full of mischief, made Steve laugh.

"*Muchas gracias,*" he said, wishing with all his heart that he could say more.

After leaving her, he joined Uncle Matt at the small hotel. They went to bed early because immediately after Steve's plane left at dawn, his uncle intended to return to the forest.

Lying there in the dark, Steve recalled the last time he'd stayed at this hotel. How frantic he had felt, and confused and scared, with Ron's package under his pillow and the man with the missing fingers waiting in San José. Everything was different

tonight. The excitement of going home overshad-
owed his sadness at leaving Costa Rica. Plans for all
that he wanted to do and to learn jammed his head.

   He thought of seeing his family again, and of how
glad they would be that he had grown into a different boy. What fun he'd have telling Grandpa about
the chickens keeping safe in the log! He remembered
how Grandpa worried about him. What Grandma
had said came back to him now: "He's okay. One of
these days he'll catch fire for something." Right away
Steve planned to tell her, "Grandma, you were
right—I caught fire! Monkeys caught me on fire!"
He pictured how her face would brighten with
surprise, and how she would laugh. And so would
Grandpa. Steve chuckled to himself stretched out
in the bed thinking about tomorrow. What a great
homecoming for an ex-couch potato!

Aileen Kilgore Henderson grew up in Alabama, where she resides in Brookwood. She served in the Women's Army Corps during World War II as an airplane engine mechanic and a photo lab technician. After the war she graduated from the University of Alabama and taught school in Northport, Alabama; Big Bend National Park, Texas; and Stillwater, Minnesota. She has worked with children and adults as a docent in historical museums, art museums, and a home for abused women and children. She is a volunteer proofreader for *Alabama Heritage Magazine* and is an active member of the University Lutheran Church. Her first book for children, *The Summer of the Bonepile Monster,* won the Milkweed Prize for Children's Literature and the Alabama Library Association Award.